THE FORTUNES OF TEXAS

Follow the lives and loves of a complex family with a rich history and deep ties in the Lone Star State

FORTUNE'S SECRET CHILDREN

Six siblings discover they're actually part of the notorious Fortune family and move to Chatelaine, Texas, to claim their name...while uncovering shocking truths and life-changing surprises. Will their Fortunes turn—hopefully, for the better?

FORTUNE'S MYSTERY WOMAN

Ridge Fortune can't believe his eyes when he discovers a woman clinging to her infant daughter on his ranch—a woman with no idea who she is and how she's stumbled onto his property...or into his life. As her memories flood back, "Hope" slowly recalls a life she just had to escape. Finally, it's time for her to stand as an independent woman. Could her new start include the rancher who's provided comfort, shelter...and, perhaps, so much more?

Dear Reader,

What a whirlwind it has been since the Fortunes of Texas hit the little town of Chatelaine, Texas, where scandals and secrets—old and new—abound!

The secrets that are locked in the mind of the young woman Ridge Fortune calls "Hope" are on the verge of breaking through the amnesia that has plagued her for months. The only thing Ridge can hope for is that those memories of her life "before him" won't take her away again when they do. Only Ridge isn't entirely innocent of keeping a secret or two himself...

I hope you'll enjoy this trip to Chatelaine and that you'll root for these two young lovers to find their way to a future together as much as I did!

All my best,

Allison

FORTUNE'S MYSTERY WOMAN

ALLISON LEIGH

THE FORTUNES OF TEXAS

Special thanks and acknowledgment are given to Allison Leigh for her contribution to The Fortunes of Texas: Fortune's Secret Children miniseries.

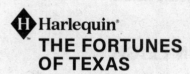

Harlequin®
THE FORTUNES OF TEXAS

Recycling programs for this product may not exist in your area.

ISBN-13: 978-1-335-99677-0

Fortune's Mystery Woman

Copyright © 2024 by Harlequin Enterprises ULC

Harlequin Enterprises ULC
22 Adelaide St. West, 41st Floor
Toronto, Ontario M5H 4E3, Canada
www.Harlequin.com

Printed in Lithuania

MIX
Paper | Supporting responsible forestry
FSC® C021394

Though her name is frequently on bestseller lists, **Allison Leigh**'s high point as a writer is hearing from readers that they laughed, cried or lost sleep while reading her books. She credits her family with great patience for the time she's parked at her computer and for blessing her with the kind of love she wants her readers to share with the characters living in the pages of her books. Contact her at allisonleigh.com.

Visit the Author Profile page
at Harlequin.com for more titles.

*For "Fortune" lovers everywhere,
including the fine authors with whom it is
my privilege to work, plus the spectacular
team at Harlequin that supports us. In particular,
thank you to Susan Litman, who manages to keep us all
on track and never seems to lose the smile in her words.*

Chapter One

The car.

It was *the* car.

Late-model sedan. Four doors. Charcoal gray.

The sun reflected blindingly off the windshield, preventing her from seeing who was behind the wheel, but it didn't matter. The car was steadily approaching. Coming her way.

Nausea clawed up Hope's throat, and sweat suddenly beaded on her lip despite the sharply cool January day. She nearly slipped when the forward momentum of her fake-leather boots stalled, and she wrapped her arms tighter around the carrier strapped against her front.

Protect the baby!

The words screamed through her head as she shrank back against the solid building next to her. As soon as her shoulder felt the contact, she whirled. The back of her winter jacket crinkled and caught against the rough brick as she rolled around to escape. Heart hammering in her chest, the recessed doorway right behind her felt like a godsend, and she ducked into it, not daring even a single glance back as she yanked at the glass-fronted door.

The jingle of bells above her head were an assault on her heightened senses despite the merry little tone of them. She started forward, but something from behind tightened around her throat.

Choking.

She gasped, taking another step, frantic to escape, but it tightened even more. She squeezed her eyes shut.

Protect the baby!

"Hold on there, hon. Your scarf's caught in the door."

She hardly heard the words over the racket of her heartbeat.

"There you go." The constriction around her throat abruptly eased, and a smiling middle-aged face swam into her vision. "That wind out there is crazy today, isn't it? Just blew the door shut right on you. Saw that right away." The woman was tugging her hood off her own head as she peered at the bundle strapped against the front of Hope's coat. "What a darling girl," she cooed. "My youngest granddaughter just had her first birthday. She was a Christmas baby. Bet you're not *quite* that old yet, are you, ladybug?" She laughed delightedly at the animated leg kicks her comment seemed to earn, and wiggled Evie's fuzzy-lined boot for half a second before she turned her smile to Hope's face.

The nausea was starting to fade, but Hope felt as breathless as if she'd run a marathon.

Not that she could remember ever running a marathon. It was just one detail among hundreds of others—like her own name—that Hope hadn't been able to recall for the last six months.

She cradled Evie's comforting weight against her but couldn't keep from looking over her shoulder back through the windows of the door.

The rear end of the dark gray car was just rolling past.

Her mouth dried all over again, even though the vehicle kept traveling, innocuously moving through the intersection.

When it had gone far enough that she couldn't see it anymore, her breath silently eased out between her clenched teeth.

She turned again and realized the lady was still looking at her, the smiling question in her eyes shaded by more than a little concern at Hope's behavior.

"I, uh, I thought I saw someone I knew," she said with too much cheer that didn't seem to fool the woman at all. "Time flies really fast, doesn't it?" she added quickly. "Evie's eight months now."

At the sound of her name, her daughter garbled nonsensically and kicked the little fuzzy boots that had been under the tree on Christmas morning just two weeks ago.

Another gift from Ridge.

He'd given Evie so many things.

Hope, too.

The knowledge was like a little weight inside. Comforting yet very, very disturbing.

At least the woman stopped eyeing her as if she suspected Hope was someone who needed eyeing. "It does go fast. Enjoy every minute of it," she said. Then she caught the little starfish hand that Evie had extended and laughed lightly. "Even more so when you get to my age." She wrinkled her nose, still smiling engagingly. "You realize it's all gone by in the blink of an eye."

"Hi, Miranda." A slender brunette carrying a stack of hardback books appeared nearby, prompting Hope to take proper stock of her surroundings.

A bookstore. Cozy. Slightly crowded. Entirely charming. Her breath evened out a little more.

"I thought I heard your voice." The brunette was speaking to Miranda. "I've got your special order in the back." Her bright smile took in Hope and Evie. "Are you here for our story hour?" She tilted her head toward the back of the shop. "They're just getting started, and we always have room, particularly for new faces. I'm Remi, by the way. Are you new in town? Visiting someone for the holidays?"

Panic had driven Hope inside the shop, not the lure of story hour. In all the months since she'd inexplicably found herself in Chatelaine, Texas, she'd only ventured into the town proper a handful of times. She started to shake her head. "I, um—"

"You should join them," the woman—Miranda—encouraged. "Nothing like forgetting yourselves in a good story hour. Remi here has amazing taste in books, whether for children or old ladies like me." She winked. "Books. Always good for what ails you."

"Truer words," Remi quipped with a smile, "but *old ladies*?" She rolled her eyes, giving Hope a conspiratorial grin. "We should all have the energy of Miranda Tibbs." She maneuvered the stack of books in her arms and extended her hand toward Hope. "I'm Remi Fortune."

Fortune.

Undoubtedly another relation of Ridge. He was almost as new to the Chatelaine area as Hope—and in addition to his siblings who'd also recently relocated there—the whole region seemed riddled with members of the extensive Fortune family.

All of whom had been nothing but kind to her and Evie.

"Hope," she returned, quickly shaking Remi's hand before resuming her usual position of cradling Evie against her. She didn't give her last name. How could she? It wasn't the first time she'd felt a moment of awkwardness from that telltale omission. One would have thought she'd have learned how to deal with it by now. "I, um, we can't stay. I'm supposed to be meeting someone at the Daily Grind."

"Maybe next time, then," Remi said easily. "We have story hour every Wednesday at ten. Mondays, too."

"Thanks." Now that she'd mentioned the coffee shop, she felt inordinately anxious to leave, so she backed up again to the front door, pushing it open with her weight. "It was nice meeting you."

"You, too, Hope."

The two women continued smiling at her as she went through the doorway, and if there was speculation in their eyes, Hope pretended not to see it.

Once outside, she turned again into the stiff breeze, pressing her lips against her daughter's silky hair before tugging the hood of Evie's tiny jacket in place. Looking over her shoulder, she searched the street for a glimpse of the dark gray sedan.

From what she could tell, traffic in downtown Chatelaine was never all that heavy and this Wednesday was no exception. Which is probably why it had been so easy to see that car.

Why had she thought she recognized it?

There was nothing special about a dark gray car. There was one right now, in fact, parked not far ahead of her in front of the feed store, and *it* wasn't filling her with the screaming meemies. It didn't have to mean there were people in town again asking questions about a young woman and baby...

So what was it about that *other* sedan?

She'd known it was *the* car. The one that Ridge's brother Nash had talked about seeing only a few months ago.

She pressed her fingers against the pinpoint of pain behind her right eyebrow. It was coming more frequently lately. Ever since she'd started getting flashes of memories.

If they *were* memories.

For all she knew, she was just losing her mind.

She blinked against the tears that threatened and ducked her head against the cold wind.

Focus. Just focus on one thing.

How many times had Ridge said those words to her?

Take a breath and let everything else go.

He could have been standing right there next to her, saying the words in his low, deep voice.

She took a deep breath, inhaling the presence of her daughter. "We're going to be fine, Evie," she murmured against the baby's slick hood. "Ridge—"

Her throat closed.

He was their rescuer. Their safe harbor. She'd known it from the moment her blurred vision had cleared on his face six months ago when she'd woken up in his stables one night with no memory of how she—or the baby who'd been crying in her arms—had gotten there.

Nothing in the time since had convinced her otherwise.

He was wonderful. Perfect. Handsome. Gentle. Kind. He never lost his temper. Or raised his voice. Evie loved him and so did—

She gave a sharp shake of her head, focused on the cracked cement sidewalk under her boots and started down the street again. They were already ten minutes late, but she knew that Ridge would just blame that on their appointment with the pediatrician's office.

Evie started fussing, and Hope quickened her pace, looking up and down the now-empty street before jaywalking across it, angling toward the bunch of vehicles parked diagonally in front of the Daily Grind.

She was jiggling the baby to no avail as she went inside, following in the wake of a wizened old gentleman wearing a cowboy hat big enough to house a family of squirrels. Her gaze immediately settled on the tall man leaning against the far side of the counter.

He'd been watching for her, too, and his smile was slow and slightly tilted as he straightened.

She kept herself from skipping—jogging…okay, *racing*—to him with an effort and tried not to fall into a pathetic heap when his focus went from her face to Evie.

"What's the matter, baby?" Ridge's eyes were as brown and delicious as a shiny dollop of dark, melted chocolate.

Predictably, Hope's mouth seemed to water and feel dry all at the same time, and only several months' worth of practice kept her from visibly reacting when his hands brushed against her as he deftly undid the fasteners of the carrier before lifting Evie out of it.

He swung the baby above his face and tilted her until her nose touched his. "What're you sounding so cranky about, Little Miss?"

As soon as he'd lifted her, Evie's fussing had magically stopped, and now her little hands closed in his brown hair— just as glossy as his eyes—and she yanked enthusiastically. "Ba-be-ba-ba!" Her fuzzy boots frog-kicked so hard that one of them flew off.

Hope laughed and caught it before it could land in someone's coffee.

And right then and there, the entire charcoal gray car reaction became a thing of the past.

Ridge was laughing, too, and he deftly twirled Evie in his arms until she was cradled high against his chest. "You're gonna roast in that thing," he told the baby, tugging off her little puffy purple coat to reveal the red T-shirt with Mommy's Bestie printed on the front. He tugged the hem of the shirt down over the slight pudge of her tummy and the stretchy denim leggings. Only after he'd dealt with Evie did his gaze finally focus on Hope. "How was the doc?"

"Fine." She took the coat from him before working the

boot back onto Evie's stocking-clad foot. It wasn't easy with the way she curled her toes. "She's grown an entire inch since her six-month checkup." Not that this was a surprise to either one of them, given the rate Evie had been growing out of her clothes.

"And the cough?"

The cough Evie's developed in the last few days was the reason for the appointment in the first place. "Dr. Monahan said she'd prescribe something if it doesn't clear up on its own, but she doesn't have an infection or anything." Hope patted her daughter's padded rump, and when her fingertips brushed accidentally against Ridge's forearm, she curled her fingers as tightly as Evie's toes. "Have you ordered?"

He shook his head, and she made a point of looking at the laminated coffee menu lying on the counter. He stood close enough that she felt surrounded by the warm scent of him. Soap. Fresh air. *Him.* "She said to call again if it worsens or starts affecting her eating and sleeping."

"Hear that?" Ridge was addressing Evie. "No more waking up at three in the morning, or it's back to the doctor for you."

"Ba-ba-ba!" The baby's blue eyes were adoring as she hung her head back, arching herself over Ridge's arm and clasping her hands together.

The empty carrier sagged from Hope's torso, and she unconsciously rotated her shoulders. Ridge was a foot taller than she was. Evie's height was no burden at all to him. "Did you get your business finished okay?" Ridge had also had an appointment in town that morning, which is why he'd said they'd meet up in the Daily Grind after.

"For now." He didn't elaborate. Not that Hope expected him to.

Yes, they had fallen into a certain familial-like routine since he'd found her unconscious last summer. But Hope wouldn't make the mistake of forgetting that they were *not* a family.

Evie had a father. He'd been Hope's husband. She was almost certain of that now, and Ridge was perfectly aware of that fact, too, since he'd been present when she'd remembered that she used to wear a wedding ring. She'd also remembered her husband's funeral. Or at least she thought she'd remembered it.

Her memories were so disjointed, she was afraid to trust anything as real. What if she was confusing real facts of the past with the jumbled dreams…nightmares…that plagued her?

Why didn't she feel *grief*? Was there something more wrong with her? Was her mind coming up with a horribly convenient way to justify the life she was living now?

Until she could trust her own mind, there was no hope of going back.

Nor any hope of moving forward.

Certainly not with Ridge.

Because as much as he adored her daughter—and everyone, including his mother and his five brothers and sisters, freely acknowledged that this was so—he'd never once crossed the line where Hope was concerned.

He'd held her when she'd needed comfort.

Wiped her tears when they'd needed wiping.

But he'd never kissed her.

Not even close.

She wasn't sure what she would do if he ever tried.

And what sort of woman did that make her?

"Decide what you want?"

She jerked slightly, looking up from the laminated menu

that was clenched between her fingers. She hadn't even realized that she'd picked it up or that she'd shoved Evie's coat into the already strained-at-the-seams diaper bag.

Her throat felt tight, and she shrugged, forcing a smile that she didn't feel. "I can't. There're too many choices." She knew the Daily Grind had the best coffee in the county, but in her heart of hearts, she was a tea girl.

He plucked the menu from her fingers. "Close your eyes."

She obediently closed her eyes.

"Now stick out your finger and point."

She pointed, feeling the slick menu against her fingertip.

"Mocha latte," he gave the order as she opened her eyes and saw that what she'd really pinned the finger on was espresso. Only he'd known better. "Americano with two extra shots for me," he added.

The coffee shop was busy, and it was obvious it would take a few minutes for their order to be prepared, so Hope headed to one of the few empty tables while they waited. She pulled off the carrier and looped it and the fraying strap of her pink-and-white-gingham diaper bag over the back of her chair before sitting down and peeling off her own coat.

Ridge had offered more than once to get her a larger, sturdier diaper bag, but she kept refusing. If it wasn't for the name *Evie* embroidered in minty green on the flap of the bag, she wouldn't even know the name of her own daughter.

Her eyes prickled, and she turned to stare out the side window. By the time Ridge joined her at the table, managing both Evie and a paper plate nearly too small for the large chocolate croissant it held, she'd banished the tears once more.

He set the croissant in the middle of the table beyond Evie's reach and tossed down a bundle of napkins he'd pulled from the pocket of his leather jacket.

Despite herself, Hope's mouth watered, and she immediately reached out to break off a corner of the warm, flaky pastry and popped it in her mouth.

The croissant was buttery. The chocolate was rich and slightly bittersweet. The combination was addictive. She reached again and her fingers knocked into Ridge's.

"Sorry," she mumbled and snatched her hand back, twisting her fingers together in a knot atop the table. Her skin hummed, feeling warm from the steady look he gave her.

"You seem antsy."

The observation didn't help her nerves. "Not at all." The lie was obvious even to her.

He shifted Evie on his lap and reached forward, settling his palm over Hope's white knuckles and pressing slightly to keep them in place when she automatically tried to withdraw. The gleam of his gold watch peeked from beneath the edge of his leather sleeve.

He was Rolex watches and designer duds, whereas she was homemade diaper bags and discounts. No matter what she remembered or didn't remember, she needed to keep that in mind.

Ridge Fortune was in a class all his own.

"Did you have another memory?"

Her throat felt tight, and there was no scarf caught in a closed door to blame this time. "No."

"But...?"

She shifted in her seat. "It's nothing." She didn't want to tell him about the car. About her illogical fear of it. But when he looked at her the way he was now, she knew from experience that she had no willpower whatsoever.

"Hope—"

"Order up for Ridge." The call came from the clerk at the counter.

Ridge's lips tightened slightly.

"I'll get it," she said in a rush and slid out of her seat.

Saved by the coffee.

Chapter Two

The drive from Chatelaine to Ridge's house on the north side of Lake Chatelaine was a little more than ten scenic miles. That morning, though, Hope's usual appreciation for the beautiful Texas landscape was absent.

Evie was silent from the back seat of Ridge's luxurious SUV; she was sound asleep and not providing the least distraction from Hope's troubled thoughts.

In six months, she'd learned more about Ridge than she had about herself. He'd always been unfailingly patient with her, but she knew even the deepest well had a bottom, and judging by the lines forming alongside his lips, she couldn't help wondering if he was reaching it.

If she told him about the car, she knew his first reaction would be to go all protective.

That had been his response from the moment he'd found her unconscious on his property. Instead of immediately calling 911 or the police, he'd called a physician friend of his. To deal with her health more immediately than the authorities... because who *knew* what situation had driven her into the horse barn of a complete stranger, with an obviously young infant strapped to her chest and no identification on her at all?

"Why *didn't* you call the police?" The words came out

utterly without thought, and she wanted to kick herself for not having better control.

He was slowing the vehicle as he turned up the road leading to the Fortune Family Ranch—which was a lot more than a single ranch to her mind, but his family could call the compound whatever they wanted.

"What?" His attention remained on the road that ran along the sometimes jagged perimeter of the enormous lake. "When?"

She glanced over her shoulder at Evie, but the sleeping baby still provided no distraction and Ridge was waiting expectantly. "When you found me." She faced forward again. "You, um, you called your friend Mitch, instead."

He didn't answer immediately, though she felt his gaze through the dark sunglasses he wore. He slowed slightly as they neared the ranch headquarters—a cluster of red-bricked barns and a long, low building that housed the offices—before picking up a little speed again as the road straightened out and moved toward the main lakeside house where his mother resided. "Mitch is the best doctor I know around here. Would you rather I'd have called the police?" he finally asked.

"No!" She shifted. "I wasn't thinking that at all," she said truthfully. "It's just not what most people would do. Most people would want to wash their hands of the situation as soon as they could."

The corner of his lip quirked. "I'm not most people."

How well she knew that.

She chewed the inside of her cheek and stared out the side window again. His family ranch numbered more than three thousand acres and employed more than a dozen people from outside the family. She'd met most of them at one point or another. Easy to do when nearly all of them lived on the property or nearby.

Once they passed the turnoff to his mother's house, the road meandered more, cresting a hill and then another before passing the first of the six luxuriously modern log homes occupied by him and his siblings. Hope knew they'd been built as guest cabins for the original owners of the ranch who'd retired to Arizona. But calling them cabins was as accurate as the whole ranch/compound thing, as far as she was concerned.

The first of them was occupied by his eldest sister, Jade, who'd established a petting zoo on the property, mostly as an attraction to get kids involved in the educational workshops she taught.

The zoo was probably Evie's favorite place in the world, and a part of her couldn't help imagining her baby girl someday participating in a workshop, too.

Wishful thinking. That was years down the line, and who knew what their situation would be by then.

The thought was still plaguing her even when they reached the turnoff for Nash's place. Nash was Ridge's eldest brother and acted as the ranch foreman. He'd always been nice to her—they all had been—but Hope had also always felt a little intimidated by him.

"I wanted to help you," Ridge finally said when they'd driven past Nash's property and were about halfway to the next gate leading to Arlo's place. "That's why I didn't call the police. Would you rather I'd have handled things differently?"

She made a face. "It would be proof of being the biggest coward in the world if I'd waited six months to tell you so, wouldn't you say?" She looked down at her ringless fingers, focusing on the memory of when that hadn't been the case. When a narrow band had adorned her wedding ring finger.

She concentrated on the image. Could almost feel the faint weight of the gold.

She curled her fingers. Trying to savor it? Or rid herself of it?

"You're not a coward."

She flattened her fingers against her thigh, looking at him from the corner of her eyes. "How do you know?"

His lips quirked again. "I just do."

"Same as you just knew I needed help?"

"Maybe."

What could she say to that?

She exhaled and looked out the side window again. They passed the stone pillars and open gate marking Arlo's property, and she mentally paced off the distance to the next gate. She knew it was roughly a mile between them. She also knew that it was almost exactly five miles from Ridge's front door to Jade's petting zoo. Even though there was a perfectly good golf cart at her disposal, Hope had probably walked the distance a hundred times now, pushing Evie in the fancy all-terrain stroller that Ridge had bought for her. His gate was as big as Arlo's, but slightly edgier with its deceptively simple bronze metal lines.

Gravel spun slightly under the SUV wheels as he turned from the paved road and drove through the opening. She'd never seen his gate closed, either. "Do you ever close it?"

"The gate?" He smiled faintly and shook his head. She wasn't sure if it was in answer to her question or in judgment of its inanity.

"When Evie's older, might have to," he mused after a moment. "Just to keep her corralled."

The notion was disconcerting.

Somehow, months had passed without her making any serious effort to leave.

Why would she when Ridge had made staying with him so impossibly easy?

She chewed the inside of her cheek again. Would she be thinking the very same thing a year from now? Two? Five? Ten?

Ridge was an eligible bachelor. The youngest son of the Windham Plastics magnate, Casper Windham. But Casper had died last year, and the company had been sold. Which left Ridge and his siblings even richer.

Sooner or later, he'd want a real family of his own.

Her stomach clenched painfully at the notion, and she suddenly sneezed, burying it in her elbow.

Dust was clouding up from the gravel as Ridge drove. He'd been talking about having the long drive up to his house paved, but so far hadn't done anything about it. She felt certain it was because he, himself, wasn't certain just how long he'd be living there.

Her life was in limbo because she couldn't remember where she *really* belonged. However, his life was too, because—so far—he didn't want to disappoint his mother who'd been the one to transplant herself and her six adult children here when she'd found herself a widow *and* an heiress to a father she'd never known.

Sooner or later, all limbo had to end.

Didn't it?

She abruptly sneezed again. Dust had always bothered her. "'Scuse me."

He pulled into the circle drive that fronted the beautiful house, with its pitched roof and wings extending from the central A-frame, and parked. "I'll get Evie and you get the door."

Since he was better than Hope at extracting the sleeping baby from her car seat—again, purchased by Ridge—she didn't argue. She gathered up the carrier and diaper bag and walked up the stone steps of the house. A swipe with the fob he'd given her months ago after installing a fancy security system and the door unlocked with a soft snick. After a nudge, the big, heavy door swung inward, revealing a view straight through the center of the house to the gleaming lake on the other side.

She didn't have to possess her memories to feel certain that her life BC—before Chatelaine—had not involved luxurious "cabins" with million-dollar lakefront views.

Evie was still sound asleep as he carried her past Hope, her lips pursed into a sweet bow and her cheeks rosy in her otherwise porcelain complexion. Hope pressed her lips to the baby's forehead when Ridge paused as he stepped into the foyer. Despite the flushed cheeks, Evie didn't feel any warmer than usual, and Hope stepped away again. She looked up at Ridge as she did so and felt her breath catch slightly when she found his gaze on her.

He'd left his sunglasses in the SUV, and his pupils seemed dilated a little in the change from outdoors to in. "Want her in her crib?"

Her throat managed to allow some nonsensical sound to escape, and she nodded jerkily.

A vertical line creased between his brows. "It would be easier if you'd just say what's bothering you, Hope. The things I'm imagining are bound to be a lot worse." His thumb brushed Evie's flushed cheek. "Dr. Monahan really said she's fine?"

Remorse was swift, and she was squeezing his forearm before she even realized it. Of course, his first thoughts were always about Evie. "Really," she assured him and by some miracle disconnected her fingertips from the roping sinew barely disguised beneath soft leather. "I would tell you."

"Then it's another memory." He waited a beat. "About *him*?"

He meant her husband. Former or otherwise. The man who'd put the wedding ring on her finger who may or may not even be alive. She sighed. The twisted memories were riddled with both love and pain. She couldn't tell which one superseded the other and that alone was tormenting.

She turned away from Ridge, tossing up her arms in defeat. "I saw the car."

"What car?"

She looked over her shoulder at him, and his lips tightened.

"That car," he muttered. "The one Nash—"

"Yes."

Ridge exhaled slowly, though he looked more angry than worried. "I'm going to put her down." He turned on his boot heel and silently disappeared down the wing where the nursery and Hope's bedroom were located.

His bedroom was on the opposite side of the house.

He wouldn't even let Hope clean over there, though she'd tried to offer cleaning house for him in exchange for the shelter he'd been giving them all this time. The end result was that she had never even seen past his bedroom door.

She knew it would be tidy and clean. The housekeeper he *did* allow to clean was named Terralee, and she kept the entire place spotless despite the presence of an eight-month-old baby.

Any other details, though?

They existed only in Hope's imagination.

She walked through the great room and around the enormous kitchen island. In the current home-designer world of white and more white, Ridge's kitchen was an entirely different animal, with the cupboards finished in a warmly muted and antiqued green, juxtaposed against caramel-colored wood counters that almost exactly matched the color of the narrow strip of sandy shoreline only yards away from the house. The result felt cozy, despite the oversize footprint and wall of windows that spanned the back side of the house.

The view wasn't merely of the spectacularly beautiful Lake Chatelaine, but of the multilevel deck protruding from behind the manor. It worked its way from a covered area, complete with two stone fireplaces, down to a dock that extended far out over the water.

Every inch of that deck begged a person to go out and enjoy it.

The pot of Irish breakfast tea that she'd brewed earlier that morning was cold, and she filled a mug and stuck it in the microwave situated below the countertop on the island. While it heated, she leaned her arms on the tawny counter and moved the small baby monitor closer. The image from the baby's room was full color, the sound perfectly clear.

Another Ridge purchase, and he hadn't skimped. There were four other monitors situated around the house and a fifth outside on the covered deck.

Everything inside her felt melty and soft as she watched him lean over the crib, gently depositing Evie onto the mattress. She squawked only once and immediately rolled onto her side, one hand going to her cheek and the other clutching the corner of a crinkly fabric book that Hope had given to her for Christmas. In the two weeks since, Evie had rarely let the book out of her sight.

Books just made Hope think of the bookstore, Remi's Reads, which just further made her think again about the car.

She turned down the volume on the monitor and, since she was able to see when Ridge left the nursery, perched herself down on a bar stool, more or less prepared for his return.

"Where?"

She didn't pretend to misunderstand. She set the mug on the counter and slowly turned it in a circle. "In front of the feed store. Before I got to the Daily Grind."

"Who was driving?"

She shook her head. "I don't know. I couldn't see."

His lips compressed. He yanked open the refrigerator door and pulled out a glass bottle of milk, taking a swig straight from it. He replaced the cap and stuck it back on the shelf.

She couldn't help staring. He bought the expensive milk from a small dairy farmer who actually delivered the stuff twice a week, and she'd never once seen Ridge do such a thing.

He turned back to her, and his lips were twisted again. "This whole situation is giving me an ulcer," he muttered.

Dismay sank through her. "It is?"

He made a rough sound. "No." As if to prove it, he grabbed the twin pot next to hers that held his black-as-tar coffee. He filled a mug and repeated her steps of heating it in the microwave. "What did the car look like?"

She told him.

"That describes probably half the cars around town."

She wanted to find comfort in that logic, but didn't. "I know it was them."

Them being the couple Nash had told her and Ridge about. Middle-aged. Seemingly nonthreatening. Yet when they'd described a woman who looked like Hope, Nash had instinctively denied seeing anyone in the area who fit the description.

In some of the worst half-dream-half-memories that tormented her, there was a couple. Seemingly nonthreatening.

Until they were.

Not for the first time, she wondered if she'd done some-thing bad.

If that was why she'd taken her baby and run. Run from her life.

There simply was no other way to describe what seemed to have happened. Hiding away in a wealthy man's stable among his prized racehorses with no identification or money on her at all. She'd been running. Either from something someone else had done, or from something *she* had done.

She inhaled shakily and adjusted the baby monitor an in-finitesimal centimeter. The perfect beauty of her sleeping baby was solidly real.

Then the microwave dinged, startling her.

She was turning into a basket case.

Hope watched Ridge remove his mug from the microwave and take a swig of the steaming contents. She couldn't help wincing just a little. Whether or not his stomach was lined with titanium, his mouth seemed to be.

"They're the only ones who've looked for you," he said. "If you were really on the run, there'd be police reports."

"Stop reading my mind," she murmured and picked up her own mug, burying her nose in it.

"I don't have to read your mind. Your face telegraphs every thought you have."

That remark was hardly comforting. Half her thoughts were about *him*. Her cheeks felt as flushed as Evie's had been, and she was grateful for the distraction of her tea.

"Remember anything else?" he asked.

"About the car?" She shook her head.

"Well. Whoever it is, they can't get to you here."

By *here*, he meant his house with the fancy security sys-tem. Even if he did start using the gate at the end of the long gravel drive, it wouldn't keep out someone who was determined to get past it. They could simply climb over.

It would be a hefty climb, but not an insurmountable one.

She tried imagining the middle-aged couple that Nash had described scaling Ridge's gate—which, at its highest point, was probably at least eight feet—and couldn't. The fencing beyond the gate pillars was just plain old barbwire. A good set of cutting tools could take care of that.

"What if they come with lawyers?" Equally worrisome.

"We have lawyers, too."

Her throat tightened. There were days and days that had gone by when she wasn't beset with anxiety. When she could almost forget that she hadn't sprung to existence last summer on this piece of Texas land.

And then there were days like today.

Which were coming ever more frequently.

"Maybe I should see a therapist," she murmured. It was what Mitch had suggested on his most recent visit. He, Ridge and several other guys had gotten together for poker just after New Year's Day. Testosterone town while she and Evie had hunkered down on their side of the house, even though Ridge had assured her that she didn't need to stay hidden away.

"If that's what you want."

She couldn't tell one way or another what he thought about it. Her facial expressions might be an open book for him, but she couldn't say the same about him. Sometimes she could read him perfectly well. Like when he was with Evie. And other times…

She sipped her tea again. What she *wanted* was the certainty that she belonged right where she was. And that wasn't going to happen regardless of what she did or did not remember. She knew more than a few things about Ridge Windham slash Fortune. Or Fortune slash Windham. Or just Fortune, if he kept to his mother's desire to embrace everything about her newfound family name, even if it meant wiping out her children's connection to their late father.

She knew he'd grown up with privilege and wealth in Cactus Grove, near Dallas. That he'd always had his pick of women—and there'd been plenty, if the gossip sites were even remotely accurate. She knew he could tolerate everything from the strongest coffee imaginable to even the hottest chili peppers served at Harv's New BBQ in town.

She knew he never lost at poker. That he could sit for hours doodling on a piece of paper and end up with some new contraption to sell that would save someone time and money. That he'd accepted this house that his mother wanted to provide him only because he loved her and didn't want to cause her more upheaval than she'd already endured, but that learning all the ropes around the ranch was a poor substitute for the engineering work he'd done for his father's company. A company that appeared to have been sold right out from under him and his siblings.

She knew that the diamond key pendant he'd given to her as a Christmas gift was little more than a trinket to him, even though she suspected the cost of it would buy her and Evie a very long way down the road if she sold it.

Which she would never do.

But she couldn't bring herself to wear the incredibly beautiful platinum and diamond pendant. Nor could she ever bear to part with it.

What she also knew was that, right or wrong, she was in love with him.

But he was *not* in love with her.

Evie? Most certainly.

But Evie's mom?

Chapter Three

Ridge watched the pull of Hope's soft pink lips as her frown deepened. "If it upsets you that much, *don't* see a therapist," he said. He knew he was equally as anxious for her memories to return as he was for them to be forever gone.

Hell of a note.

Her lashes swept down, hiding the periwinkle blue. "I'm just afraid of what my brain isn't willing to give up. What could be that bad?"

She wasn't quite telling the truth. He could see that, but he couldn't *really* read her mind. His mom had always told him he was too intuitive to waste himself on engineering. He'd always considered the combination of the two made him better at each.

He was good at figuring out things, but he'd definitely dragged his feet where Hope was concerned.

Sure, he'd monitored every news feed he could find for details about missing women matching her description. He'd even hired a private investigator—something that he hadn't admitted to a single one of his family members. The only one who knew was Beau Weatherly, who'd recommended Gordon Villanueva in the first place. Ridge's meeting that morning while Hope had been at the pediatrician with Evie had been with Beau.

Not at the coffee shop, though.

Just because the retired rancher and investor placed a mildly tongue-in-cheek sign out on a table in the Daily Grind most mornings offering Free Life Advice didn't mean that Ridge intended for his personal business to be discussed in public. But there was no denying that the man unfailingly had sensible advice.

Despite Ridge's efforts, though, he'd only met dead ends. Whoever *was* out there looking for Hope wasn't doing so because of a missing person's report. Not in the state of Texas, anyway, where he had limited the search at first.

As soon as Ridge had hired him four months ago, though, Villanueva had expanded that territory into the surrounding states, and more recently the entire country.

There had been three women fitting her general physical description with criminal charges of child abduction—all of which the investigator had determined were unrelated.

Until the middle-aged couple that Nash had come across, there hadn't been a single person out there seeming to make a diligent effort to find her. And so far, Gordon Villanueva hadn't been able to locate the couple, either.

Ridge never doubted that Evie was Hope's biological child. They shared the same birthmark on their necks. It was small, but distinctively star shaped. In the months since he and his sister Dahlia had found Hope in his stable, Evie's hair had come in even more, just as auburn as her mother's. And though he knew the color of babies' eyes often changed, it seemed to him that Evie's were only becoming more periwinkle blue like Hope's.

Evie was Hope's. Unquestionably.

But who else's was she?

The specter of Evie's father—Hope's husband—was always

there. Had he died? Or was Hope's memory as faulty as she feared and he was still alive?

If he was and everything had been normal and fine in their marriage, why hadn't the man been turning over heaven and earth to find them? Even if their marriage hadn't been happy, what about the baby? If he wasn't alive, why had she run? What did she have to fear?

Ridge felt Hope's gaze on him, and he realized he'd been rubbing the pain in the center of his chest that was a constant companion whenever he speculated on the circumstances that had brought her and her baby into his life.

Circumstances that would take them away again.

He pushed away the annoying thought. He'd had plenty of practice at it since last summer, but since Christmas, it was getting even harder.

He never should have given her that necklace.

Because now he kept noticing how she never wore it.

She was still watching him with a slightly pinched expression, drawing the corners of her lips down.

"Don't suppose you got a license plate or anything on the car?"

She was shaking her head before he finished speaking, her frown deepening. "I hid in a bookstore," she admitted huskily. "A total coward. I should have—" She broke off, pressing her lips together.

He set down his coffee mug and went over to her, dropping his hands over her shoulders. "It's okay," he murmured. He squeezed slightly, and her head tilted, resting against him. She exhaled softly, and the pressure in his chest grew. His jaw tightened until it ached. "It's okay," he said again, more firmly, before releasing her.

Nash hadn't gotten a license plate, either. Just the description of a late-model gray sedan. Of which hundreds of thousands were purchased every year.

"I'll see if there is a therapist Mitch recommends," he said, picking up his coffee again and moving around the island, well away from the lure of touching her. "You can decide if you want to pursue it or not."

"Okay."

But still, the white edge of her teeth worried at her lower lip. Then she shifted as though she was shrugging off a weight, and her gaze skipped around the kitchen. "Aren't you supposed to be working this afternoon?"

He glanced at his watch. "Yeah." The farrier was coming that afternoon, and Ridge was supposed to meet her down at the main barn. He worked his head around, trying to loosen the tightness in his shoulders. "I'd better change. What about you?"

Hope picked up the baby monitor and showed him the screen. Evie was awake. Lying on her back and kicking her legs while she chewed on the corner of her fabric book. "I figure I have two minutes of grace before her contentment disappears," she said wryly. "Just enough time to make you a sandwich if you want one."

A part of him wanted to blow off the farrier and the ranch altogether, just to stay there with her and the baby. "We still have leftovers from that roast you made?"

"Yes, including a few slices of the sourdough loaf I squirreled away before you could eat it all."

Now the corners of her lips were tilting a direction he far preferred. The slight smile always struck him as slightly impish, whereas a full-on smile from Hope pretty much felt like a celestial event.

She set down the monitor and slid off the bar stool, and when she moved past him toward the refrigerator, he breathed in the scent of her hair. He was twenty-nine years old. He didn't know if she was eighteen or twenty-five. He seriously doubted she was older. There wasn't a single line on her youthful face.

"I'll change," he muttered, and escaped the kitchen. His bedroom was at the end of the opposite wing, and he made short work of exchanging what were dress clothes for him these days for old jeans, work boots and a flannel shirt. Gone were his days of bespoke suits, high-rise Dallas offices and manufacturing plants, though half his closet was still filled with those suits.

When he returned to the kitchen, a fat plastic-wrapped sandwich was sitting on the island next to the baby monitor, on which he could see Hope changing Evie's diaper. The sound had been turned down, and he thumbed the button until he heard the sound of her softly singing to the baby.

You are my sunshine, my only sunshine…

A fresh pang in his chest, he turned down the volume, took the sandwich and left the house. Bypassing the SUV, he ate as he walked past the pool and the small guesthouse that was on his property, and headed toward the barn and stables that were only a fraction the size of those located at the ranch headquarters.

He stopped long enough to check the water and feed the three retired racehorses he hadn't been able to give up when he'd moved from Dallas. He called 'em Larry, Moe and Curly. Their official registrations, however, were Toddy Boy, Winter Sun and Ali of My Heart. They had forty-nine starts between them and over a million in winnings. Now they were out for stud.

"Living the dream, right, guys?" He rubbed their foreheads one last time, tossed the plastic wrap in the trash barrel and climbed behind the wheel of the dusty pickup truck he used while he was working around the ranch. A wind was kicking up, and it blew through the passenger window that would no longer roll up all the way. He pulled out the puffy vest that he kept stuffed behind the seat along with an assortment of other handy items and put it on before starting up the engine.

The steering was a little loose and the shocks were almost shot, but he did find something vaguely satisfying about driving the thirty-year-old bucket of bolts. It was a helluva change from the sports car he'd driven in the city. And though money had always been easy in his life, he couldn't see plowing through creeks and muddy bogs with the Escalade that had replaced the Porsche.

He drove through the gate, smiling a little to himself despite the restlessness that had plagued him ever since his mother purchased the property last summer.

The ranch had already been a fully functioning cattle operation when they'd taken it over, lock, stock and barrel. Since then, Ridge had been learning all there was to learn by working alongside the fifteen employees who did everything from cooking to cowboying.

Not because he figured he'd ever be running the place.

Nash had already staked out his position as foreman, and once his older brother decided on something, that was all there was to say about it. Sabrina handled the books. Arlo was already a successful investor and was busy turning around ranches that were failing—which was not the case with the Fortune Family Ranch, as it was known now—and Jade and Dahlia were doing their own thing and were all about the animals. Jade with the nonprofit petting zoo she'd established, and Dahlia raising sheep of all things, right in the middle of a cattle ranch.

Ridge was the youngest of them all and the only one who

didn't have a place where he actually belonged. And unlike Dahlia and Jade, he couldn't see inventing—or reinventing— himself.

He was an engineer, for God's sake. He'd figured his place was at Windham Plastics.

His father had had other ideas, and in the months since the company had been sold, Ridge had faced the fact that his father would have felt that way even if he hadn't been stricken down by the pancreatic cancer that killed him.

Casper hadn't been an easy man. He'd been cold and distant. To his wife and to his children.

The only time that Ridge had felt like he and the old man were even close to being on the same page was when Ridge worked at Windham Plastics. But where his interests fell more heavily on solutions for the healthcare industry, Casper had chased the best profits. Period.

None of Ridge's brothers or sisters had wanted to work at Windham. Only Ridge had. And despite the battles he'd had with the old man, in the end—despite being blindsided by Casper's decision to sell the company to his biggest competitor—Ridge had made his peace with him.

The company's not for you, Ridge. Those were the last words his father ever said to him. *Find out what is.*

A day later, his father was dead.

Ridge didn't think he was going to find out what "it" was by stringing fence and learning the ins and outs of cow-calf pairs.

But he also had Wendy to consider.

Ridge knew his parents' marriage had been far from perfect, but she'd still been rocked by Casper's death. And it was obviously important for her to make a connection to this Fortune side of her family that she'd never known existed, or she would never have thrown herself so precipitously into this new life. As a parent, she was the opposite of Casper, and she wanted her offspring along for this new ride.

As much as Ridge wanted to find "it" for himself, he wanted to see his mother happy. She, more than anyone, deserved it. For all the disappointments they'd suffered with Casper as a father, Wendy had been the opposite. Ridge couldn't count the number of times his mother had kissed him good-night. "Good day, bad day," she'd whisper, smoothing his covers even as she tugged away the building blocks he'd usually been clutching, "you are loved, and love is everything."

He automatically turned onto the frontage road leading to the headquarters and returned Sabrina's wave from where she was standing in front of the offices talking on her cell phone.

He could see the farrier's trailer before he reached the barn. He parked alongside Nash's truck and went inside. He figured the only reason Nash—four years older than Ridge—didn't give him a censorious look for being ten minutes late was because he was busy jiggling the crying baby he was holding.

Ridge was still trying to get used to the idea that Nash was a father, much less that he'd so readily given up his long-standing insistence that fatherhood was *not* for him. But there he was, carrying around a bundle of baby who was about the size now as Evie had been when Ridge first discovered Hope in his stable.

Mentally tabling his intention of rehashing Nash's initial encounter with the gray car and the only people on earth who had seemed to want to find Hope, he stopped next to his brother and peered into the wailing, unhappy face of his nephew. "Colt is giving you quite a ride, I see."

His brother shifted the baby to his shoulder, patting his back through the snug swaddle of pastel blue and green stripes. "You'll never make it in comedy, dude. Stick with the day job."

Ridge grinned a little and turned to greet Lucille, the sixty-some year-old farrier. Her hair was as bright a red as Lucille Ball's had ever been, and he couldn't help speculating whether or not the deliberate color choice was because of the name. Not a person to waste time or mince words, she was already hard at work, and even though he was only a few minutes late, he could see she was already cleaning and trimming the fourth hoof of Goldie, one of the oldest horses they had. Goldie was also one of a handful of horses that were shod. She would be getting a new set of shoes today, which lengthened the period of time Lucille would have to spend on her. For those horses that went barefoot, it only took her about twenty minutes to clean and trim their hooves.

In addition to Goldie, though, there were eleven other horses that Lucille would see that afternoon, and it was Ridge's task to make sure all of them were ready. All but three of them were still out in the pasture, and he started gathering up halters.

"Imani busy this afternoon?" Nash was engaged to Colt's mama, and even though Imani Porter ran her own successful specialty baby gear company, it wasn't that often that Nash brought their son to work.

"She and her mother went to Corpus for the day." Nash repositioned his son again, trying the pacifier that was fastened to his blanket with a bright red clip, but the infant wanted nothing to do with it.

Ridge couldn't help feeling a little pleasure over his brother's awkwardness. It wasn't often Nash seemed out of his element. But Ridge also knew very well that sense of helplessness.

Just because Evie wasn't his by birth didn't mean he loved

her any less, and the worst thing he'd ever felt was not being able to soothe her when she'd needed soothing and Hope wasn't there to do it.

"Try flipping him over," he advised. "Hold him like a football." He mimed what he meant before heading down the aisle between the empty horse stalls toward the opened doorway on the opposite end that led to the nearest of their pastures.

A whistle brought three quarter horses immediately toward him, and he led them into their barn stalls with ease. He might be an engineer, but he'd still been around horses for most of his life, and remembering that he liked caring for and riding them as much as he liked racing them had been welcome. Every time he could feel his stress level where Hope's situation was concerned, hands-on time with the horses had proved a good way to help dispel it.

Nowadays, instead of recreational romancing, he was practicing recreational horse maintenance.

The gossip rags back in Dallas who'd loved recounting his social life would have had a field day with it.

Eyeing his big brother, Ridge was pleased to see that Nash was holding the swaddled bundle of his son like a pro footballer, his big palm seeming to be exactly the cradle that Colt had wanted for his head.

"It's something about the pressure on their bellies," he told Nash as he grabbed a few more halters from a peg. "Worked great with Evie, too." He raised his voice a little to be heard over the loud sound of Lucille working a red-hot horseshoe over the anvil.

The noise wasn't bothering Colt at all.

His eyes were closed, his lashes long and dark against his pudgy cheeks, his pink lips drawn up in a bow like he was nursing in his sleep. Meanwhile, Nash was staring down at him with naked adoration.

Was that what Ridge looked like, too, when he held Evie? Probably.

He just hoped that emotion wasn't so obvious to everyone and their mother's brother when he gazed at Evie's mother.

He went back outside. Gathered up two more horses, though he had to do a little chasing this time. Despite the cold wind, the vest was no longer needed, and he pulled it off and hung it in the tack room when he got more leads.

Lucille worked thoroughly, but fast, and if he didn't want to be outpaced by a woman older than his own mother, he didn't have time to lollygag. By the time he'd gotten the rest of the horses stalled, she'd finished with Goldie and three more horses, and Nash had taken the baby inside the ranch office.

Ridge kept himself busy in the barn while Lucille worked. She couldn't abide someone hovering over her and there was plenty of grunt work for him to take care of while still making sure the next horse was ready and waiting when she was ready.

She worked steadily, breaking only when her equine pedicure client needed a break. By the time she was finished and he had turned all the horses back out to the pasture, he couldn't understand how she could even stand up straight. Farriering was backbreaking work.

But she did stand straight and give a cackling raspy laugh when he pointed it out. "Sonny, I'd rather do *my* work than yours."

That was true. At least *she* had a purpose.

He helped her load up her equipment and opened the door of her dually pickup for her. "Nice manners," she said as she heaved herself up onto the high seat. "Be back around next month," she told him and drove off just as the sky opened.

He watched her taillights wink through the drenching curtain of rain.

No purpose. But good manners.

He supposed things could be worse.

Chapter Four

It was nearly dark when Ridge let himself into his house through the back door of the laundry room.

The rain had let up, but only slightly. He pulled off his boots and grabbed a few towels from the stack that Terralee had left folded on a shelf. Then he proceeded to mop up the puddle of rainwater he'd made on the floor with one and raked the other over his head. He could smell something good coming from the kitchen, and his stomach growled right on cue.

Ridge yanked the wet flannel over his head without even bothering to unbutton the shirt and tossed it into the deep sink next to the washer and dryer that were so modern he didn't have the first clue how to run them. The shirt landed with a wet slap. If he didn't have to walk through the kitchen and the great room, he'd have left his soaking jeans there, too. Instead, he peeled off his socks and added them to the pile, then, with the towel hanging around his neck, he walked barefoot into the kitchen.

He'd expected the usual sight of Hope and Evie—bright eyed and pink cheeked as she smashed some unidentifiable substance against the tray of her high chair—but he stopped short at the sight of his sister Jade sitting at the big island, too.

She was Nash's twin, but the resemblance stopped at their

coloring. Nash liked being captain of everything. Jade, however, rivaled Ridge when it came to blending into the background among the rest of their siblings. Funny, really. The eldest and the youngest sharing the same trait. But since starting up the zoo and becoming engaged—for real—to Heath Blackwood, she'd seemed to come into her own. She'd obviously found the "it" that Casper had told Ridge to find.

The basset hound by her feet was the same as always, though, and Ridge leaned down to scrub Charlie's ears on his way to peek at whatever deliciousness was happening on the stovetop. So what if his arm happened to brush against Hope's when he lifted a lid on a big pot to look?

She avoided making eye contact with him as she waved the wooden spoon to keep him at bay. From the soup or from getting too close to her was up for debate.

"It's minestrone," she said. "And it's hot." Another wave of the long-handled spoon, this time aimed even more directly at him. Her blue eyes looked at him and skittered away as fast as a drop of water on a screaming hot pan. "You'll burn yourself."

Too late. Since he'd met her, he'd been on a long walk to incineration.

But he knew enough to focus on the here and now. And right now meant the aroma coming from the pot. "Smells great," he said truthfully. Whether or not Hope ever remembered her entire past, she was a terrific cook and seemed to relish pouring over cookbooks and trying out new recipes.

It was a good thing he was working his tail off physically around the ranch. If he hadn't been, he'd be wearing a larger size by now for sure.

He grasped the ends of the towel hanging over his chest just to make sure he didn't do something stupid, like grasp *her*, and caught Jade's measured gaze.

Probably thinking she could read his mind.

She, like the rest of his family, had embraced Hope and the baby. They all shared that same protective instinct that had kept Nash from admitting anything to those strangers. But Jade also was clearly worried what it would mean for Ridge when Hope's memory *did* return.

For once, though, his sister held her tongue about the matter, but only because both Hope and Evie were right there.

He moved over to Evie and, thanks to weeks of practice, was able to avoid her grasping, sticky hands as he leaned down to kiss the top of her head. She babbled nonsensically and slapped her hand down on the goop on her tray, obviously delighted at the way it splatted out from beneath. Then she immediately lifted her hands, her eyes sparkling up at him.

To hell with a little sticky gunk.

He lifted her out of the high chair and laughed when her hands went right to his hair. "Messy girl." He blew a raspberry against the polka-dotted shirt that had replaced the red one from that morning, and she gave a belly laugh that wrapped him right around her sticky little fingers.

He nuzzled her warm cheek and slanted his gaze toward Jade. "Where's Heath?"

"He had a business meeting at the LC Club this evening." Heath was something of a wunderkind in the agriculture and tech field. Self-made, successful and only a year older than Ridge. Which also made him three years younger than Jade. But there was no reason to suspect that Heath was after Jade for her money, because he already had plenty of his own. "And then he's hoping to meet the triplets for a drink afterward."

The triplets were Heath's half sisters. All of them had been separated as babies and reunited only recently. Proof that Casper Windham's family wasn't the only screwed up one around these parts.

"I came over to see you about this." She was fluttering a simple embossed white card between two fingers.

"If that's a new wedding invitation for you and Heath, fine. But if it's that strange one we got last month—"

"Heath and I haven't set a date yet." Her cheeks flushed a little as she spoke, like she couldn't quite believe *she*—a tomboy according to their late father, who'd never find a man—was getting married.

She squared up the rectangular wedding invitation on the counter. The invitation had been preceded each month with one oddball request or another back to July when they'd all received the initial save the date.

Unfortunately, neither the first missive nor any of them since gave them a clue to the identity of who was actually getting married. Which, as far as Ridge was concerned, was a good enough reason to ignore the whole thing despite his mother's insistence otherwise.

"There's a rumor that you're not planning to attend the mystery wedding," Jade said.

Ridge glanced down at the likely culprit to spread that news. "A rumor, huh?"

Hope didn't meet his eyes as she lifted Evie out of his arms. Her knuckles brushed against his bare chest before she turned quickly away. "She's a mess." She sounded a little breathless. "I'm going to pop her in the tub real quick. Turn off the soup so it doesn't boil over. It'll be ready soon as I add the *ditalini*." She practically jogged out of the kitchen.

Jade was still watching him.

Waiting.

"I told Hope I didn't see the point of going to a wedding where we don't even know who the bride and groom are," he admitted gruffly. "Nothing I haven't said before." He turned off the stove burners.

"Ummm." Jade pressed her lips together for a second. "Think you were supposed to leave the one under the pasta going."

He made a face and took a minute figuring out which switch controlled the right burner.

Jade was rolling her eyes when he'd completed the task. "For Pete's sake, Ridge. How'd you fend for yourself before Hope came along?"

"I was still in Dallas," he reminded her.

"Oh, yeah." She wasn't impressed. "With a new date every night of the week."

"Not *every* night." But when he wasn't going out, he'd had a housekeeper who'd kept him in meals that usually just needed a minute or two in the microwave. He wasn't sure he'd ever had cause to turn on his own stove and honestly couldn't remember if the thing had been a gas monstrosity like the one he had now, or if it had run on electricity.

He'd had meals regardless, and beyond that, he just had not cared.

He stepped over Charlie, who'd camped his sturdy self directly in front of Ridge, and ran the end of his bath towel under the sink faucet, using it to wipe the drying goop—banana, he realized—off his chest and his chin. "Why does it matter to you, anyway?"

"We've *all* been invited. It's not like it's a fluke. A misdelivery or something." She waved the invitation between her fingertips again. "Back in July when the first save the date came, I agree that it was easy to just dismiss. I mean, who sends out a wedding notice and leaves off the identity of the people getting married? It seemed like a mistake. But since then?" She shook her head. "It's obviously intentional."

"Inexplicable, you mean."

"Inexplicably intentional," she returned, ever the more-knowing big sister. "We're supposed to provide a meaningful photograph." She ticked off one finger. "Then be prepared with a meaningful quote." She ticked off another. "And the text messages?"

At one point, everyone in the family had gotten text messages like some damn survey, asking which of the example wedding attire they preferred. A, B or C.

They weren't living in some television game show, but every time one of those mystery-wedding missives showed up, it felt like it.

The text had sparked quite a discussion among his sisters and his mother. As far as Ridge knew, his brothers had ignored responding the same way he had.

"The wedding's this month," Jade said. "Three weeks from Saturday, to be specific."

He squinted at her. "Think I've got to see a man about a horse that day."

She let out an exasperated tsk. "You know that Mom wants us all to go. Present our united support."

United *front*, maybe. But Jade, like all the rest, knew their mother was his Achilles. "Go for the jugular, why don't you?"

She lifted her shoulder. "Whatever works. *Obviously*, the bride and groom are from around here. We have Fortune relations coming out our ears. Some we haven't even met yet." She tsked again and leaned toward him over the massive island. "It's a few hours out of your Saturday. Don't be like Dad, Ridgy Rigid. Come on."

He gave her a look.

"I call them as I see them, brother mine."

"If I was as rigid as he was, I wouldn't be living here." He raised his arms, encompassing the lavishly appointed home.

"As if you don't *like* living with Lake Chatelaine right outside your back door," Jade chided.

"You know what the problem is? All of you girls have weddings on your brains."

"That's kind of the normal thing that happens when you fall in love for keeps. And it isn't just the twins and me." The twins being the *other* set of twins—Sabrina and Dahlia. "Arlo and Nash are chomping at the nuptial bit, too."

The topic was wearing too thin for Ridge's comfort. There was only one wedding that he cared about these days. The one wedding he dreaded knowing more details about.

Hope's. To another man.

He flipped the towel back around his neck. "If I say I'll go, will you get off my back about it?"

"I haven't been *on* your back," she said sweetly. "I *could* be if—"

He staved off her words with his hand and nearly tripped over Charlie, who'd moved again to lie right under Ridge's feet. He leaned over and rubbed the dog's head. "Dude. You know how to pick the spots, don't you."

"This says to bring your plus-one." Jade propped the invitation against the mason jar that was filled with the remains from a fancy Christmas bouquet that Ridge had bought for the holiday. "I assume that plus-one won't be Terralee."

He nearly snorted. Terralee Boudreaux was a bold-as-brass transplant from New Orleans who was twenty years older than him. "She'd make mincemeat out of me."

"Whereas Hope won't?" His sister's voice was soft and abruptly serious.

"Leave it alone, Jade."

She sighed audibly but didn't press. "So, you'll go. Both of you. What about the photograph thing?"

"What about it? Think I'll be kicked out if I show up

without one in hand?" He tossed up his hands. "I'm not one for taking pictures. You know that." He didn't even keep photo albums.

"You take pictures of your engineering—" she swizzled her fingers in the air between them "—thingamajigs all the time."

"Designs," he deadpanned. "They're called designs, Jade."

He was earning the eye rolls from her big time.

"Whatever." She slid off the bar stool and patted her thigh. "Come on, Charlie. Let's go home and wait for Heath."

The dog lumbered to his feet. He was so short legged, his long ears practically dragged the ground. But he gave Ridge's bare foot a drooly swipe of his tongue as he headed toward Jade.

"At least your dog loves me," Ridge told her.

Her lips stretched. "I love you, too, you big dweeb." Her gaze flicked toward Hope's wing of the house. "I also worry about you."

"You don't have to."

"Might as well ask the moon to stop rising every night."

"Speaking of the moon." He followed her to the doorway. "There isn't any moonlight out there with the rain." He flipped on the exterior light, but the circle of illumination that it cast reached only as far as the wide shallow steps that led up to the front door. They glistened wetly. "It's dark as hell. Sure hope you drove over in something better than that golf cart you use at the zoo."

"That golf cart has headlights *and* fog lights," she returned. "Which is more than I can say about my real vehicle." Jade patted his cheek before scooping Charlie up in her arms and skipping down the steps.

He watched her jog through the rain—now more a drizzle

than a curtain—and disappear into the dark. A moment later, headlights beamed out from what was obviously the golf cart.

The headlights were better than nothing, but even after she'd driven out of sight, he still felt like he should have driven her home.

"Jade decided not to stay for soup?"

He nudged the door shut as he turned to see Hope coming into the room. Evie was clean again, her damp hair glossy and dark and slicked back from her forehead in a tiny little ponytail that stuck nearly straight up. "Yeah. She wanted to get home to Heath."

Hope's lips twitched. "Can't really blame her there."

She missed his grimace because she was leaning over, deftly spreading a jungle-themed baby quilt on the floor. Then she set Evie down on it with her favorite chewy book and some big plastic keys on a ring before going to the kitchen. She checked the pasta in the pot, adjusted the burner and turned to wipe down Evie's high chair with a wet cloth.

Hope had a graceful economy of movement and he could always tell when she was flustered because that's when that economy faltered.

"Are you, uh, going to clean up before we eat?"

He usually took a shower and shaved before sitting down with the ladies for dinner. But since he'd had a shower thanks to nature, he shook his head. The way her gaze slid to his bare chest prompted him to at least go and put on a clean shirt.

When he returned to the kitchen, she'd tucked the high chair away in a narrow alcove between the fancy built-in gas stove and a tall glass-front cabinet. She jumped a little when he pulled out the bar stool and turned away from the glass. Almost as if she'd been using it to check her reflection.

Despite himself, he reached for the wedding invitation sitting against the jar of still-piney scented twigs. Pressing it flat with two fingers, he slid it a few inches back and forth on the satiny wood surface while he watched Hope stretch up to pull two wide, white soup bowls from inside the cabinet. The action stingily revealed a narrow swath of creamy skin between her jeans and her dark blue sweater.

The invitation bent slightly under the pressure from his fingers, and before he did more damage to it, he stuck it against the mason jar again. Then he folded his arms, leaning on them against the island. "I think the price of you spilling the beans to Jade that I didn't plan to go to this thing is for you and Evie to come with me."

The slotted spoon she'd picked up banged against the side of the pan, spilling water down onto the hot burner. "I don't have anything suitable to wear to a wedding." She started to turn toward the sink, checked the motion and then turned back again to the stove. Dipping the spoon in the pot again, this time she successfully transferred the helping of pasta into one of the bowls. She followed it up with a ladle full of soup from the other pot.

He picked up the invitation yet again and tapped the edge on the counter. He absently adjusted a piece of greenery in the mason jar. "It's at the Town Hall," he said. "Two in the afternoon. Hardly black tie." He slid his glance her way. "The dress you wore at Christmas was—" *Captivating.* He cleared his throat a little and set aside the invitation before reaching for the bowl she set on the island for him. "It would work fine."

He reached over and pulled a soupspoon from the drawer of flatware. "For that matter, what you're wearing now would be fine."

She stopped halfway between the stove and the island and gave him a look. "I may not remember the mascot from Central High, but I *know* this—" she spread her arms and looked down at herself "—is *not* appropriate wedding guest attire." She looked up again and flushed slightly. "What?"

"Did you hear yourself?"

Her lovely lips pressed together. "Yes, I heard myself. And don't pretend that *you* were raised to think that frayed blue jeans are appropriate for a wedding." She faced the stove again with her ladle and the second bowl. "At least one that isn't being held on some mountaintop," she added in a scoffing manner.

"Central High," he repeated. "That's what you said."

It took a moment, but then her shoulders visibly stiffened.

The bowl clattered a little when she set it back down on the counter next to the stove. "Central High," she said softly. Wonderingly.

She angled her head slightly and closed her eyes, obviously concentrating. "The home economics teacher was Mrs. Jones. No. Johnson." She shook her head again. "That's not right, either. Something like that. But it was my favorite class." She gave a faint laugh. "Because it was easy."

Ridge was already thumbing his phone, running a search for Central High School. Dozens of locations came up. Not just in Texas but in the surrounding states. He was afraid of pushing Hope for more details, though. It had never been successful in the past and usually ended up doing more harm than good, leaving her drained and disappointed.

It was hard, but he took the opposite tack. "Soup's really good. Minestrone's one of my favorites."

"Your mother told me." She sounded absent as she picked up her bowl again, added pasta and then the aromatic, vegetable-studded soup.

She carried it to the island and took the bar stool next to him. "Jenson. Jordan. What *was* her name?"

"It doesn't matter," he said. Even though it did. Any piece

of the puzzle of her past was invaluable. "When were you talking soup with my mom?"

"A few days ago. She came by with another outfit for Evie. I told her she had to stop buying clothes for her, and she said she'd picked it up for nearly nothing at a thrift store." She made a sound. "As if your mama *ever* shops in a thrift store."

"She wasn't always wealthy," he replied mildly. Wendy Wilson had been raised in near poverty in Cactus Grove, believing herself to be the daughter of a single mother named Gertie Wilson. Poor or not, though, she'd been an honest-to-goodness Texas beauty queen who'd caught the eye of Casper Windham, and from then on, poverty became a thing of the past.

But his mother had never forgotten the value of a hard-earned dollar. And now, she knew the truth about Gertie. That she'd only been Wendy's babysitter when Wendy was an infant, left in her care by her real mother, who'd perished in the same terrible mining accident sixty years ago that had claimed the lives of fifty miners.

With nobody else coming forth for the baby, Gertie had taken the baby away from Chatelaine altogether and raised her as her own in Cactus Grove.

All of which had come to light bare weeks after Casper's death, when Wendy learned the truth about her real family. Both her parents had died in the mine accident. But her maternal grandfather was a millionaire named Wendell Fortune with plenty of secrets in his own life, not the least of which had been faking his own death for many, many years, riddled with guilt over the mine tragedy that had also claimed the life of his secret, illegitimate daughter. He'd left the country, only returning a few years ago, but even then, he'd used an assumed name until his failing health prompted him to begin fessing up to his remaining family.

But there'd still been a missing puzzle piece—the baby of the daughter he'd never had time to publicly acknowledge.

He finally located her—Wendy—shortly before his ill health claimed him for good. Wendell's bequest to Wendy?

A castle.

Turrets and all.

Located just outside of Chatelaine.

Now, Ridge's in-with-both-feet mother was embracing her newfound Fortune roots and remodeling the castle into a boutique hotel. She'd gotten all six of her adult children to move to town along with her, and he was still sort of shaking his head, wondering exactly how she'd accomplished it.

"You should know by now that when Wendy Fortune has her mind set on something—even if it's baby clothes—she's not going to let anyone get in her way," he told Hope.

"A trait she seems to have passed on to all of you."

And yet, she'd stayed with Casper. From the time Ridge was old enough to realize that there seemed little love between them, he'd wondered why she had never left him.

"Well." He got up to refill his soup bowl and glanced over at Evie, who was still chewing on her book, but only half-heartedly since she was nearly asleep. "I'm set on you and Evie making that infernal wedding tolerable. I couldn't care less what you decide to wear, but you've got three weeks to figure it out."

Her lips tilted, but there was an air of sad confusion in the faint smile. "Why do you do all of this, Ridge?"

He felt his chest hollow out a little. "You don't really want me to answer that, do you?"

A flush blossomed over her cheeks and her pupils seemed to flare for a moment.

Then Evie let out a loud squawk.

Hope's throat worked and her gaze dropped away from

his. "I need to feed her and put her down," she murmured, as if she needed to explain, even though this was their usual routine and had been for weeks. She slid off the bar stool. "I'll clear up all of this later."

He watched her collect Evie and the blanket and head out of the great room.

And he continued watching long after he heard the soft sound of a door closing.

Central High.

It was a start.

Chapter Five

"I've checked seventeen schools between Texas and New Mexico," Gordon Villanueva reported two days later, "with Central in the name."

Ridge could hear the squeak of a chair through the phone and easily pictured the investigator sitting in the battered chair at his Corpus Christi office.

"I know you estimated Hope to be in her early twenties," Villanueva said, "but to cover our bases, I added another seven years to the window. But none of the schools had a home economics teacher with a last name starting with *J* during that period."

"What if she was wrong about the teacher's name?" The way she'd spoken about the school had been entirely unforced, unlike the name of her home economics teacher.

"Anything's possible. Which is why I still have my assistant tracking down yearbooks. I've sent you what we have so far because it'll take a helluva lot of time going through them manually to see if she's a student in any of them. But in the meantime, while she works on the rest, I'll start on states east of Texas. The term 'Central High' covers a lot of possibilities, but we'll get there."

Ridge propped his arm on the top of the handle of the post-hole digger he'd been using and squinted against the sunlight. The rain from two days ago was gone, but it had left unseasonable warmth and humidity in its wake.

There was nothing around him except a few head of cattle. Jaime, who'd been working with him earlier, had needed to run home to take care of his toddler son because their usual babysitter had flaked out and his wife had a meeting she couldn't miss.

Ridge hoped the ranch hand wouldn't be gone the rest of the day. The fence they'd come out to repair had turned out to be worse than expected. If he had to do it all alone, it would take him twice as long as expected. And he'd have a long walk back to his pickup truck at the ranch headquarters since Jaime had taken the work truck.

He swiped his sweaty forehead with his arm and switched his cell phone from one hand to the other. "Money's not an object. If you need to bring more people on to help—"

Villanueva's laugh was almost as raspy as Lucille's. "Already done that. I know you're champing at the bit for answers, Ridge. This is the most concrete information we've gotten. But it still takes time. Eliminating seventeen possibles narrows the remaining field. You should have the first box of yearbooks today or tomorrow. Maybe Hope looking through them will shake more memories loose. But if they don't, we'll still get there."

Ridge squinted even more. Once they did "get there," what was he going to do about it?

"And if she remembers any other details, no matter how small, let me know." The investigator rang off and Ridge pocketed his phone.

He looked at the holes he'd already dug for the new line of fence and angled his head, eyeing the invisible line where he still had to dig a half dozen more. Only a handful of days after a rain, but the ground was as unforgiving as if there'd been no rain at all.

While he didn't necessarily mind the physical work, the drawback was it left his brain plenty of time to roam. And not even imagining a half dozen ways to make the process more efficient was enough to keep his thoughts from turning back to Hope.

Eventually, Jaime returned, muttering complaints about wives and kids and the cost of everything under the sun.

He didn't seem to need any input from Ridge, which was good, since his experience with any of that was nil.

By the time they planted the remaining posts and finished stringing the wire, the sun was giving out. Jaime dropped him off at the office and drove off without delay. It was Friday, and for him, the end of a workweek.

Ridge, on the other hand, went inside long enough to grab a cold drink. Sabrina was still at her desk, her blond head bent over her work.

"Aside from it being past quitting time, shouldn't you be sitting somewhere with your feet up or something?" She still had a few months to go in her pregnancy, but she was carrying twins and was—in his inexpert brotherly opinion—sporting a whale.

She smiled at him and leaned back, showing that she did, in fact, have her feet propped on a cardboard box of files underneath her desk. "I'm just finishing up the payroll for the week," she told him. "Zane's picking me up soon. We're having dinner at the LC Club."

"Nice."

"I think so. What's this baloney about you not going to the big mystery wedding?"

He eyed her over the cold can of soda. "Where'd you hear that?"

"Jade."

Naturally. All his sisters were uniquely different. And nonetheless thick as thieves. "Is there anything the three of you *don't* share?"

She lazily smoothed her hand over her ginormous belly, and the sapphire engagement ring on her finger winked under the fluorescent lights. "Oh," she mused, her eyes looking suddenly…feline-ish. "There might be a few details."

He held up his hand. "Just stop there. I don't want to know."

Sabrina's smile widened mischievously. "You think you're the only one of us who gets to have a sex life?"

"Gack." He pulled a face.

She laughed and pulled her feet off the box, sitting up to the desk as much as her pregnancy allowed. Then she plucked a perfectly sharpened pencil from a pencil cup. It exactly matched the other dozen pencils still in the cup, not to mention the one that was already tucked behind her ear. "If you're just going to stand there drinking a root beer, find somewhere else. *I* still have work to do."

"I told Hope I'd go but only if she and Evie come, too," he admitted without having any real intention of divulging anything.

Sabrina raised her eyebrows slightly. "Was there ever any likelihood of you going *without* them?" She pulled a sheaf of papers off the printer adjacent to her desk and placed them precisely on the blotter in front of her. With one eye on him and one on the papers, she ran the tip of her pencil down the printed columns, checking for God only knew what. Her progress halted only once. She circled something, turned the page over and gave him a look, as if she was still waiting for an answer to what he'd considered a rhetorical question in the first place. "Don't pretend you're not falling for her. We've all seen it."

He ignored that. "She made some comment that she doesn't have anything suitable to wear."

His sister's eyebrows rose again. "There's nothing in my closet that would work for her," she stated the obvious. "Even from before these two soccer stars growing inside me. Hope's tiny. I'm the Jolly Green Giant standing next to her."

It was an exaggeration, but only slightly. Pre-preggers, Sabrina had been just as slender as Hope. But Sabrina was considerably taller. "I was thinking something more like a shopping trip."

She still looked uncertain. "You think she's not going to find it odd if I approach her out of the blue for a shopping trip?"

"She won't think it strange if you tell her you're shopping for something for the baby girls there." He gestured, taking in the jut of her belly. When she was still deluded enough to think that she and Zane could just share parenting duties when it came to their children without her falling head over heels for him, she'd done a stint of babysitting for Evie. "Tell her you want her advice or something and you can slide in the wedding part."

"Well." Sabrina absently tucked the pencil behind her ear, dislodging the first one, which slid behind her to the floor, unnoticed. "It's not a bad idea. Whenever I start looking at all of Imani's stuff that she carries at Lullababies, I want everything under the sun, and I *know* we don't need that much. Zane didn't become responsible for his brothers until they were already adolescents, so he's new at this whole part of things, too."

"Just don't forget it's not all about you," Ridge reminded.

"I know. Wedding guest attire." She plucked another pencil from the cup and pointed the pink eraser tip at him. "Who do you think you're talking to here? But as it happens, what I *thought* I'd wear is already getting too tight to accommodate these two—" the eraser tip aimed toward her belly "—so I actually ought to get something as well." She flipped the pencil again, swirling it dismissively in the air at him. "Now get out. I don't want to be late meeting my fiancé."

He left and was just passing Arlo's gate when his cell phone rang again. Answering, he heard Beau Weatherly's deep voice boom through the cab. "You alone?"

It wasn't Beau's typical greeting, and Ridge felt a surge of anticipation. "Yeah." Even though he knew nobody would likely overhear, he still rolled up his truck windows and turned down the volume a little. His foot eased up on the gas pedal until he was barely rolling along. "What's up?"

"Have a friend in the probate court. Nonny Zazlo's spread's going to be approved to sell in the next week. Maybe two, depending on the judge's schedule. That's one of the ranches I was telling you about last week. The one on the other side of Chatelaine. About thirty miles out." Beau cleared his throat. "House leaves something to be desired, but the land is in good shape. Excellent carrying capacity. Reliable water source. Good forage. If you're really serious about buying your own place, you could do a lot worse. Nonny sold off all the livestock when he first got sick, but he didn't have a chance to get around to selling the equipment. So, it's all going to be available, too."

Ridge's hands tightened on the steering wheel. Adrenaline shot through him, and he started to pick up speed again. Almost from the very beginning, he had confided to Beau that he wasn't entirely set on accepting his piece of the Fortune Family Ranch. Not when he couldn't figure out how in hell he was contributing in any meaningful way. He wanted—

needed—something of his own. His father had recognized that, too, before his death.

If Ridge had a ranch of his own, he'd sink or swim on his own.

Problem was, land in these parts was pretty locked up. Wendy being able to buy the ranch had been divine timing, both for her and for the former owners who'd moved to Arizona. The employees who already worked there were a mix of day hands who helped keep the ranch side of things working—like Jaime—a few office workers, kitchen help and a crew of all-around handymen and women who could put their hand to nearly any task, whether it was keeping the roads graded, fixing toilets or setting out spring plants around the main house.

As far as he was concerned, the place was top-heavy with employees, but he knew Nash didn't necessarily agree. And it was a given that their mom would never think of cutting down the payroll. The only time she'd give someone the axe was if they did something outright unethical or illegal.

Ridge's needs were a lot simpler, however. He didn't need a lakeside compound complete with a half dozen guesthouses or a weighty payroll. But he also wanted more than a little spit on the ground with barely enough room for a few head of cattle and a chicken coop.

He wasn't looking for a hobby. He was looking for a *life*.

"You think it'll go quick?" he asked Beau.

"Let's just say it'll be a miracle if Zane Baston doesn't snap it up before the probate clerk types up the sale approval." Beau's tone was dry.

Sabrina's fiancé was well-known for his ability to sniff out desirable parcels of land. If he wasn't an entirely decent guy who'd adjusted his entire life when he'd become guardian of his younger siblings, he'd have probably been reviled for it as much as he was admired.

That was the nature of success, it seemed.

One person loved you for it.

Another person hated you.

Ridge turned through his gate and felt the crunch of gravel under his tires. Through the darkening evening, he could see the welcoming glow of lights coming from the house up ahead.

If he bought a place of his own, would Hope and Evie even still be here to share it with him?

"I can finagle a look-see if you're intrigued," Beau offered. "Properties like it are getting as rare as hen's teeth around here. We've got more time with the other property I mentioned if you're concerned with the short timeline."

The other ranch on Beau's radar was located in Oklahoma. A lot farther away. It was larger, but less expensive. The house and barn had also burned down a while back, meaning a lot more work would be required.

"I don't want word getting back to my mother," Ridge cautioned. The other man knew perfectly well that Ridge didn't want to chance upsetting Wendy. "She's had enough to deal with this past year without worrying about my defection from the family compound."

"I've met your mama a time or two." Beau's tone remained dry. "Seems to me you might be underestimating her a mite. I think y'ought to just tell her what's in your mind."

"On the other hand, I've been her son my entire life," Ridge countered. "You don't know her like I do. She has a smile that's as sweet and agreeable as lily of the valley. But get past the pretty flowers, and a person's smart to exercise caution."

"Your mother's not toxic." Beau suddenly sounded a little

testy. Not surprising. Most every male who ever encountered his mother tended to get protective. Even though Ridge was no different, he also recognized the fact that his mother was probably the least likely person to need protection, whether provided by her sons or the local wise man.

"Not saying she is," Ridge answered easily. "But she's got a will of iron and a way of getting what she wants without seeming to lift a single one of her elegant fingers. Probably be good to remember that when she's involved with local charities and such. She'll have you offering up your wallet *and* begging her to please take some investments off your hands, too, while she's at it."

Beau let out a bark of laughter. "Yeah. Well, mebbe I can sort of see that. She sure is wrapped in a pretty package, though. So, I can set up a time for you to see Nonny Zazlo's old place if you want. I'll just make sure they think *I'm* the one interested in it."

Ridge smiled ruefully. The retiree could talk about Zane's propensity for buying up property, but Ridge knew that Beau had a nose for wise investments, too. It had made him a very wealthy man—probably more so than ranching ever had. "Just don't make them think you're too interested, or the price'll go up even more just from the rumor of it." He had his own financial resources, but they were no match for Beau Weatherly. Or Zane, for that matter.

He parked in front of his house, his gaze following Hope, who was visible through the front window as she moved rapidly around the great room, doing something that he couldn't make out. "Go ahead and arrange it. Sooner the better as far as I'm concerned."

Beau rang off, and Ridge went inside the house.

The sound of his entry was masked by the loud song that Hope was singing, and he realized then what she'd been doing. Singing "Skip to My Lou" and skipping around with Evie in her arms like they were square dancing.

He leaned against the doorjamb, watching silently. His smile widened when she hit the words *my darlin'* with particular enthusiasm and spun on her stocking-clad heel, spotting him halfway around.

She skidded slightly, and he launched forward, prepared to catch her and the baby, but she righted herself first with a breathless *"oofph!"* and Evie chortled with delight.

"I didn't hear you come in," Hope admitted. Her cheeks were rosy, whether from her square dancing or getting caught at it.

Either way, he couldn't have gotten the smile off his face even if his life depended on it. "Square dancing, eh?"

"Teach them young, that's what I've always heard." Her chin had a little bit of a point to it, and when she angled it upward like she was doing, he imagined fairy-tale elves dancing in some woodland glen.

The fancifulness of his own thoughts was almost excruciating. But he still couldn't stop grinning at her.

It had been that way almost from the first.

He reached out, realized he'd been about to tuck her glossy auburn hair behind the pretty shell of her ear, and instead, lightly tweaked Evie's button of a nose. She beamed at him, and even through the drool he could see the edges of her two upper teeth.

"They finally cut through, eh?"

Hope nodded, huffing out a puff of air that stirred the disheveled locks straying across her forehead. "Finally. Maybe now she'll sleep more than three hours at a stretch at night."

Evie stretched her arms toward him, nearly launching herself out of her mother's arms, and Ridge quickly caught her, trying not to get distracted by the soft curves under Hope's long-sleeved T-shirt along the way.

He propped the baby high on his chest and dabbed her wet chin with the candy-cane patterned drool bib fastened around her neck. "Let's see those choppers, baby girl." He tickled her chin easily into another happy grin, and she showed off the stubs of her lower teeth as well as the new teeny, pearly edges poking through her upper pink gum. Her bluer-than-blue gaze was fastened on him as if he was the most fascinating thing she'd ever seen. "Are you going to give your mama a break now at night?"

Ridge could count on one hand the number of times he had *not* awakened to the sound of Evie stirring in the middle of the night. Twice, he had made the mistake of shuffling across the house in the dark, and both times were seared into his memory.

Hope, dressed in a thigh-length nightie that one of his sisters had provided in those early days when all Hope had besides Evie was a diaper bag and the clothes on their backs, leaning over a hastily obtained bassinette while the small lamp in the corner of the room made the nightie nearly transparent.

And the second time before Christmas, when he'd had an unreasonable panic attack at the sight of an empty crib on the baby monitor, and burst into Hope's bedroom, afraid he'd find her room empty as well.

Only the two of them had been curled together on Hope's bed, both so deeply asleep that neither one of them had awakened despite his noisy clumsiness.

That had been the night after she'd remembered wearing a wedding band on her finger.

He'd leaned against the doorjamb, one hand pressing against the train charging inside his chest until it slowed.

Knowing he couldn't stop her from leaving if she decided to, whether she went because of her memories or not.

Ridge had finally gone back to his own bed, but it had been a long time before he'd slept.

He still found himself waking in a cold sweat most nights, padding out to the kitchen to check the baby monitor and assure himself that the two females who'd turned his world upright were exactly where he wanted them to belong. The only reason he didn't keep a monitor right in his bedroom anymore was because it had started to feel uncomfortably voyeuristic.

"I have fantasies about sleeping the whole night through." Hope's voice lured him outside of his head again.

Evie was blinking her ridiculously long eyelashes as she continued gifting him with her beatific smile.

Hope's expression, however, was entirely rueful. "I can't really remember what it feels like, and—" her fingers flitted with the tendrils of hair drifting over her temple "—it has nothing to do with the blank space up there."

Evie suddenly decided that twisting her fingers in Ridge's hair was a brilliant idea, and she started yanking away like a bronc rider, squealing with such fierce delight, he couldn't help laughing despite the sharp pain.

"Aww, baby." Hope quickly reached up to disentangle her grasp. "You're going to leave a bald spot," she tutted.

Ridge winced, more from the feel of her breasts pressed against his arm than the damage the baby might cause. In pure self-defense, he bent away from her, extending his arms in an abrupt game of airplane until Evie could no longer reach his head at all.

He zoomed her through the great room, not stopping until he was next to the fireplace that—for the first time since New Year's—was cold.

"I made enchiladas for supper," Hope said, seeming not to have noticed his physical reaction as she went into the kitchen and peeked quickly into the oven. "They still have about ten minutes to go if you want to clean up first." She rolled the high chair out of the alcove and over to the island, looking at him expectantly.

"Yeah." He pivoted Evie over to the high chair, tucked her in and gave her the crinkly fabric book that he found half hidden in the couch cushions before heading to his bedroom.

Sabrina had joked about having a sex life, but his had been stored in cold showers for months now.

When he returned, freshly showered and barefoot but dressed in jeans and the plaid flannel shirt that "Santa" had magically left under the Christmas tree for him, Evie was flinging puffs of cereal from the tray of her high chair, and they were landing on the large packing box that was now sitting on the floor near her.

"A courier just dropped it off," Hope answered his questioning look.

"The yearbooks," he realized aloud.

"Yearbooks?"

He hadn't told Hope about Gordon Villanueva before, but it was obvious he would need to, now.

What he didn't expect though was the way her face tightened when he admitted to hiring the investigator to help in his search for answers about her past.

She shook out a clean dish towel with a sharp snap, folded it in fourths and left it on the island before picking up a quilted pot holder shaped like a daisy and turning to the oven. "You've been working with him for four months?" She extracted the pan of enchiladas and thumped it down on the folded towel. The daisy pot holder was tossed down beside it, and it slid across the island, falling onto the floor on the far side.

He narrowed his eyes. "Why are you upset?"

She propped her hands on her hips and directed her attention at her feet. She took a few breaths, and he wondered if she was counting to ten. Or even twenty.

When she finally lifted her head, the color that had filled her cheeks had subsided, though the stretch of her lips still looked annoyed. "It would have been nice to be informed."

Hope pulled open a drawer, then grabbed flatware and two folded cloth napkins. With deliberate care, she placed a knife, fork and spoon on each before turning back to the cabinets and pulling down two plates that she set beside the napkins. She dished up several enchiladas, steaming hot and covered in dripping, melted cheese, and transferred them to one of the plates. Then carried it to where he sat at the end of the island, set it in front of him and handed him the napkin and flatware. As soon as he took them, she turned away. "If you were anxious for me to go, you should have just said so."

He reached out and grabbed her arm, stopping her before he even thought about what he was doing. "I *never* said I was anxious for you to go."

She pulled on her arm and gave him a look over her shoulder when he didn't release her. Periwinkle blue had turned to bruised navy. She tugged again, prompting him to let her go, and circled her arm with her hand as if he'd marked her. Though he knew he had not. "Then why didn't you tell me?"

"Because I was afraid of what I'd find."

Her lashes fell, casting dark shadows against her pale skin. "Then you do have doubts about me."

He muttered an oath. "I have doubts about the reason you ran!" He shoved his damp hair back from his forehead. "Was anyone abusive?"

She shook her head. "No."

"How do you know? Have you remembered something you haven't told me? Why are you so fearful of the people in the gray car? Are they your parents?"

"I don't know!" She dropped her hand and went over to Evie, who'd started fussing.

"I *said* I would talk to a therapist." Evie started crying in earnest, and Hope lifted the baby out of the high chair. Hushing her softly, she pointedly stepped around the big box on the floor.

How had the evening devolved so rapidly?

"Where are you going?"

From behind, her shoulders looked rigid beneath the bounce of her hair as she ambled away. "To take care of my baby."

He'd have had to be deaf to miss the emphasis on *my*.

Ridge grimaced and kicked the big box with his bare foot.

All it earned him was a stubbed toe.

Chapter Six

Knowing she was overreacting didn't make it any easier for Hope to conquer it.

He'd hired a private investigator.

She carried the wailing Evie into the nursery and sat with her in the upholstered rocking chair in the corner of the room, next to the multipaned window that looked out over the moonlit lake.

The frantic rocking eventually soothed Evie out of her crying, but it didn't help Hope at all.

Her gaze swept around the room. The walls were painted a soft beige with a hint of pink that was repeated in the pattern of the artfully faded rug covering most of the wood floor. Wainscoting behind the beautiful blond-wood crib was painted a rich forest green that complemented the long leaves of a six-foot ponytail palm, potted in an ivory pot as wide around as a wine barrel.

Softly colored artist prints of giraffes and monkeys hung on the walls, and a stuffed gray elephant that was as tall as Evie sat in one corner of her crib. On the opposite side of the room, an oversize woven basket contained at least two dozen stuffed animals. There was everything from a cartoonish alligator to a sheep, like those that Dahlia was raising, to tigers and lions and a zebra with a bright red ribbon tied around its tail.

She pinched the bridge of her nose, willing away the sudden burning of tears.

It was a rare week when Ridge didn't come in without some new addition for the jungle collection.

It could have been a nursery in a magazine. Designed for beauty but even more so for the burgeoning imagination of a child.

Her child.

She didn't doubt for a second that the room would have remained a perfectly attractive guest room if there'd been no Evie.

The nursery had a spacious Jack and Jill bathroom that connected on the other side to Hope's bedroom, which was exactly that. An attractive guest room, with every convenience a person could want, right at their fingertips. From the luxurious bedding on the wide bed to the television that was cleverly disguised as a mountainside painting, until you turned it on and the painting disappeared as if by magic.

If she'd found herself rescued by someone in a single-wide trailer with no luxuries beyond running water, would she have been convinced so easily to remain?

She knew she needed to face Ridge and apologize for overreacting. But she put it off.

First, she bathed Evie, even though she didn't really need it that day. Then she changed her into her footie pajamas, nursed her, read two board books about a curious penguin named Monty, and finally laid her in the crib, though she'd fallen asleep long before the second penguin book.

She went into the en suite, angled the door into Evie's bedroom to prevent the light from disturbing her and tidied up the mess left over from the bath. And she spent much too long staring in the mirror at her reflection, seeing…what?

Last summer, Ridge and Dahlia had found her in his barn,

unconscious and collapsed against a hay bale. Only later did they figure out that she'd hit her head on the middle wood rail of one of the horse stalls, and that was only because Ridge had gone looking, determined to figure out if the wound on her head was caused accidentally or from something more…nefarious.

He'd found a smear of blood, though, on the underside of the wood that seemed to imply she'd been crawling between the slats.

To hide inside the stall or to get out of it was something they wouldn't know until she remembered.

Now, Ridge had a security camera installed in the barn. But back then, there'd been nothing.

When she'd regained consciousness, she'd known what month it was. What day, even.

She knew with unshakeable certainty that Evie was her baby. She just couldn't remember the actual event of giving birth any more than she could recollect how she'd come to be inside the barn in the first place.

She knew how to fry an egg and bake a loaf of bread. But when it came to any personal details, whether as momentous as giving birth or as insignificant as her favorite flower? She'd been a total blank.

She knew. She knew. She knew.

But the most important things? She didn't know at all.

Hope finally tugged down the hem of her blue sweater, turned away from her reflection and forced her feet to carry her back to the great room.

The only thing left on the kitchen island was the stalk of lavender she'd placed in the mason jar that morning after she and Evie returned from their daily walk. The casserole dish of enchiladas was cleared away. No plates in the sink. Oven turned off and the high chair tucked in its usual alcove.

Ridge was sitting in the middle of the wide leather couch that faced the fireplace. Aside from the dimmed light fixture hanging over the kitchen sink, a lamp on the end table provided the only other illumination in the room. The courier-delivered box was on the floor next to him.

Opened.

She walked up behind him and saw the stack of high school yearbooks on the coffee table. He held one in front of him, slowly turning the pages.

"I'm sorry."

He angled his head slightly in acknowledgment. His fingers turned another slick, oversize page covered with dozens of small square headshots of high school students. "I'm sorry, too. I should have told you."

She chewed the inside of her lip, studying the back of his neck. At the way his glossy brown hair whorled slightly. Not exactly a curl but not exactly a wave, either.

Pushing her fingers into the front pockets of her jeans, she slowly walked around the couch. There was plenty of room on either side of the couch to join him, but instead, she perched on the edge of one of the squarish side chairs that sat adjacent to it.

She clasped her hands in her lap. Her heart was beating so hard, she could hear it pounding inside her head. "Why didn't you?"

"Because I was afraid of how you'd react."

She chewed the inside of her lip again.

"I didn't want you to bolt."

"I wouldn't have."

His fingers pinched the corner of the page, and he slowly flipped to the next. "We'll never know, I guess."

She untwisted her fingers and rubbed her palms down her thighs.

"You should eat something," he said. "Enchiladas are in the fridge."

The thought of food made her stomach twist. "It's not the fact that you hired someone to help find out who I am that upset me," she said slowly. Feeling her way carefully as much for herself as for him. "It's that you didn't tell me before. It felt—" She searched for an adequate word. "Bossy," she finally settled on.

He stopped his thorough perusal of the oversize book he held and looked at her. The lamp was on the other side of him, which meant his face was more in shadow than not. But she could still feel his gaze like a physical thing.

She moistened her lips. Swallowed past the irritating lump in her throat. "You made a decision that affects me without—"

"Consulting?" His tone was less than encouraging.

"Giving me the courtesy of *sharing* the information," she finished.

"Potay-to, po-tahto," he muttered and flipped another page.

"It's easy for you to say. You have all the control!" She pushed restlessly to her feet.

He closed the yearbook and tossed it onto the coffee table. "What the freaking hell do you mean by that?"

She huffed and spun around, spreading her hands. "Have you ever had to accept someone's charity?" She huffed again and turned once more, pacing across the generous space between the coffee table and the fireplace wall. "Of course you haven't. You're Ridge Fortune Windham. Owner of racehorses and inventor of—" she waved her hand "—whatever that gizmo was you invented for your father's company."

Ridge felt like ants were crawling beneath his skin. He remained seated only through sheer willpower. That "gizmo" was changing a small but incredibly relevant part of the medical plastics field. And the patent for T349, which naturally had been held by Windham Plastics, had been sold off along with everything else. It didn't matter that Ridge had been paid handsomely along the way. It was the way his father had done it that still burned even after Ridge had more or less made his peace with Casper before he died.

The way.

Suddenly, the starch drained out of him, and he sank back against the couch cushions.

High-handed.

Bossy.

He scrubbed his hand wearily down his face. Jade joked about him being Ridgy Rigid. Was he really more like Casper than he thought?

"I was trying to protect you," he said again and lifted his hand, staying, when her soft lips opened again. "But I was also—" dammit, the truth tasted sour "—trying to accomplish something nobody else was." It was the reason he hadn't told his family, either. All of them worried about him, and he was determined to prove they didn't need to.

He could take care of himself *and* the females living under his roof.

Hope's lips closed again. Pressed together for a long moment. Then she sighed faintly and moved from the chair to sit on the couch.

The thing was huge. There were still two solid feet separating them, but it felt like the world shrank a little with her beside him.

"I've never looked at it as charity," he admitted thickly.

"And I've never seen it as anything but," she countered. When she turned to look at him, there was a sheen in her eyes that made him hurt inside. "You won't even let me do the housekeeping here—"

"Hold it." He cut her off. "It's not true that you don't do

your share." He patted his stomach. "I've never eaten as well as I do now."

"It's not the same. I have to cook, anyway."

He shook his head. "Sweetheart, you and I are going to have to agree to disagree here, because we are not ever going to be on the same page about it. But if it makes you feel better, you can start mopping the floor to your heart's content. I don't care! What I care about is that you're safe and healthy and—"

Not going to leave.

He propped his elbows on his knees and raked his hand through his hair. "I'm not trying to be high-handed, Hope. I'm just doing the best I can here."

She inched closer, but only—he realized—so she could reach the yearbook he'd tossed aside. She sat back again and rubbed her thumb against the cover. It was embossed and designed to look like leather, he supposed.

"Central High," she said. "Bodecker, New Mexico."

"There are seventeen Central Highs just among Texas and New Mexico," he shared the detail that Villanueva had given him. "These are the yearbooks from the years when you might conceivably have attended from only eleven of the schools."

She looked at the large box. It was filled almost to the top with yearbooks. "How many—"

"More than a hundred. This is only one of many boxes the lawyer is sending."

She blew out a soundless whistle. "Good grief."

"If we knew exactly how old you are, it would help trim the number, but since we don't—"

"Maybe I'm older than you," she said.

He smiled a little at that. "I'm more on the hopeful side that you're at least legal to drink," he admitted gruffly.

Her eyes widened. "Of course I am."

He just looked at her. "And you know this because…?"

Her lips parted. Closed again. "Because I just do," she finally said. "I was married, for heaven's sake. That I'm sure of. I've been here for six months. Based on Evie's development, the pediatrician is fairly certain that she's about eight months old now and—" she broke off, eyes narrowed in thought "—and I remember when I was first able to vote in the *last* presidential election and thinking how stupid that I was finally legal to drink while kids three years younger were getting to help decide the leader of the free world and—"

He cut her off, laughing despite himself. "Would've been helpful if we'd have figured *that* out before now."

She spread her hands. "Better late than never, right?"

"And you—" he closed his hands around one of hers and squeezed "—must be at least twenty-five."

Ridge hadn't thought it was bothering him so much that it was technically possible that she could be so much younger than him, but judging by the almost comical relief he felt…

He blew out a long breath, but even as he did so, he was becoming aware of her palm pressed against his. In an instant, he was less interested in breathing easier than he was the feel of her warm skin. The curve of palm. The slide of fingers against fingers.

His gaze traveled down her arm. Her impossibly narrow wrist. The long, slender fingers.

He heard her inhale on a quick hiss, and slowly—so slowly it was almost painful—her palm slid away from his.

The loss shouldn't have left him aching, but it did.

She was inching along the leather couch again, only this time putting more distance between them as she tapped the year embossed on the cover. "This one is too old." Her voice sounded husky, and he ached a little more.

Setting the book off to one corner of the coffee table, Hope began checking the others that he'd already gone through, separating the *possibles* from the *impossibles*.

He got up and grabbed the ones that she'd eliminated.

"Where are you going?" she asked.

"Getting 'em out of the way." He didn't look at her, turning swiftly around the side of the couch opposite her and dumping the stack on the corner of the kitchen island. Then he headed into the laundry room on the pretext of getting a beer he didn't really want from the spare fridge out there, threw open the door and stepped outside into the chilly night.

It wasn't a cold shower, but beggars couldn't be choosers.

He walked around to the deck and twisted off the bottle cap, tossing it down on one of the side tables situated artfully around the spacious deck. Exhaling deeply, he went down the six steps to the lower level and leaned against the railing. The lake was large enough that it created its own breeze, and he was grateful because it increased the cooling effect.

As long as Hope didn't join him, he'd be fine.

If she did—

He clamped down on the thought. Having a closer idea of her real age would be extremely helpful in the investigation, but it didn't change anything else. Her ties to her past were still too much a mystery.

Ridge decided the beer was a good idea, after all, and tipped the bottle to his lips, taking a long, needy drink.

Far out in the lake, the water rippled black and shimmering beneath the moonlight. Fish jumping. Maybe someone out on a boat, stupid enough not to have a light going. He'd seen worse.

He stiffened when he heard footsteps and turned to see Hope, wearing her puffy coat, making her way down to the railing beside him. The same moonlight that glistened on the water shone on her head, picking out an occasional strand of auburn-hued hair and turning it almost gold. But her expression was a pool of mystery.

"You okay?" Her voice was soft.

"Peachy." He lifted the beer again and took another draught. Then he tilted it toward her, offering.

Her fingers brushed his as she took the bottle. "What is it?"

"IPA I discovered at the LC Club."

"I don't usually drink beer."

"How do you know?"

She gave a muffled laugh. "True." She lifted it and took a sip, placing her mouth right where his had been.

Desire stirred all over again.

She pressed the back of her hand to her lips and quickly held up the bottle for him to take again.

He deliberately brushed his hand over hers as he took it.

Masochistic, but did he really care?

"It's from a brewery called Fortune's Rising."

"Is the name a coincidence or yet another thing that your family is into?"

"Distant cousin, I think. The brewery is in Rambling Rose. Do you know the town?"

She shook her head, and he could hear the soft swish of her hair sliding over her coat. Then she pulled something from her pocket, and he realized she'd brought one of the baby monitors with her. She shared the screen with him, catching Evie in the act of turning around until her feet were where her head had once been. "She's a traveler," she murmured and tucked the monitor back in her pocket.

"It's a few hours from here. Rambling Rose."

"Oh?" She sounded only mildly interested, but something kept dogging him to continue.

He leaned his arms against the railing again, which brought

him much closer to her level. He could angle his head and look right into the pale gleam of her elfin face.

"It's not a sprawling metropolis, but it's bigger than Chatelaine."

"Everywhere is bigger than Chatelaine," she said dryly.

For some reason, that remark managed to derail his odd discomfort. This was the woman who'd been sharing his home for six months. Sharing his life, whether they called it that or not. "But we still have a castle," he defended.

She shifted, and he could feel her against his shoulder. "That's a whole weird story, isn't it? Who builds a castle in a place like Chatelaine?"

"My great-grandfather, evidently," Ridge said. "And only my mother would decide to turn it into a spa and boutique hotel."

She laughed softly, and every nerve in his body seemed magnetized toward her.

"Now we're part of this family that has members far and wide. And in my head, I'm still—"

"A Windham."

"Yeah." He took another drink and offered her the bottle again.

She accepted it even though she made a face. "Maybe it's easier not remembering than knowing you have so many connections you don't know, anyway." She made a sound. "That sounded convoluted."

He still thought he understood.

Without drinking, Hope set the bottle on the wide wood rail and held it there. "It's amazing here, you know. You and your brothers and sisters all have houses right on the lake. But—" she shifted again, and he felt the press of her shoulder even more against his "—you can't even see their places. It's like you have this piece of the world all to yourself."

"True." The meandering, sometimes jagged shoreline meant absolute privacy, unless there was someone on the lake itself. "Can stand out here stark naked if I want."

She made a sound. Maybe a laugh. Or perhaps a groan. He wasn't sure and he didn't care.

"*Do* you?" she asked.

"Not so far." His hand covered Hope's, and he straightened, pulling her around to face him. "But privacy does have its advantages."

Her hair stirred in the breeze as she looked up at him. "It does?"

"Definitely," he rasped. With his free hand, he slid her hair out of her face. Tucked it slowly behind her ear.

She swayed a little. "I think…" She trailed off when he brushed his lips over her temple.

"You think…?" He kissed her smooth cheek. Slowly slid his lips toward her ear. Her hair smelled like spring. "What?"

But she didn't answer with anything except a quick inhalation as she angled her head, but not toward escape at all. He felt the press of their clasped hands against his chest. The beer bottle was hard and intrusive but everything else about her was soft and inviting.

"Ridge," she whispered.

"Yeah?" He slowly meandered from her ear along her jawline. His fingers explored the shape of her neck where her pulse beat almost frantically.

"Nothing." Her other hand closed over his shoulder, her fingertips flexing against him. She tilted her head, allowing him better access to taste that throbbing pulse that so intrigued him. "I just like your name."

Draping his arm against the small of her back, he pulled her closer. Whatever common sense he once possessed was gone. "Then say it all you want." His mouth found hers, lifted right to his as if she'd only been waiting.

He was vaguely aware of the bottle sliding from between them and excruciatingly aware of every other thing about her. From the way she tasted to the way her fingers traveled just as greedily as his. It was only when he pulled her down with him onto one of the deck chairs that he realized the fumbling motion she was suddenly making wasn't directed at him, but at pulling the baby monitor out of her pocket again.

Then he heard it. Evie crying. Not just a little cry that would quickly abate as she settled herself again. Nah. This was the kind of cry that meant "I'm awake *now*." And it brought him back to his senses with the gentleness of a sledgehammer.

He started to set her from him. "I'm sorry," he said gruffly. "I shouldn't have—"

But Hope was already levering off the chair even without his help and taking the steps to the upper level of the deck two at a time. "I'm coming, baby," he heard her say to the monitor.

A moment later, all he heard was the slam of the side door as she went inside.

He exhaled noisily and stared up at the man in the moon. "You look like you're laughing," he accused.

The moon just continued to look back at him.

The laughter didn't stop one little bit.

Chapter Seven

"**R**eally?" Sabrina stood in the aisle of a Corpus Christi GreatStore and eyed the small box that Hope was holding up. "A manual breast pump? Everyone I know says to get one of those electric ones." She pointed at the display of breast milk pumps.

"I had an electric one," Hope said. She waggled the small box she was holding. "*This* one never lets you down. Doesn't take up half the space in your diaper bag. Doesn't wait until you have a convenient electrical outlet nearby." She shrugged. "But you know. Get both. You'll decide for yourself what works best." And goodness knew that Ridge's sister could afford to buy whatever she wanted. Her budget was undoubtedly unlimited.

As it was, she was still surprised that Sabrina had asked for Hope's help to start outfitting the nursery for her and Zane's twins. She could have just as easily asked Imani Porter, who was Nash's fiancée after all and the owner of Lullababies, which *catered* to people in their economic stratosphere.

The closest Hope could get to anything the high-end specialty baby store carried was a cutout from one of their chic catalogs.

Not that Imani herself was as snooty as some of the clientele that Hope felt certain shopped at the exclusive boutique.

She was incredibly warm, and Hope knew that Ridge's family were all happy that Nash and Imani were together again after a six-month-long breakup. But Hope was *also* certain that Ridge's mother didn't drop by Nash and Imani's home with thrift-store finds for baby Colt, no matter how perfect their condition. Hope doubted a single thing touched Colt's beautiful skin that wasn't curated from the Lullababies collection.

Sabrina, on the other hand, was all about the numbers. Regardless of her own wealth, or that of her fiancé, she must like a bargain.

It was the only explanation that Hope could think of that made sense of this little excursion that Ridge's sister had talked her into. She'd even roped in her mother to babysit Evie for the afternoon.

"It'll be our girls' afternoon out," Sabrina had said when she'd picked up Hope in her fancy SUV.

"You know they pretty much carry this same stuff at the GreatStore in Chatelaine," Hope pointed out as she followed Sabrina, who was pushing the cart up one aisle and down the other as they picked out baby bottles and burp cloths and breast cream. "We could have saved ourselves the hour drive here."

"I know, but I fancied a trip where everyone I run into isn't someone who wants to ask me about Mom or the castle or how does it feel to learn I'm a Fortune." Her smile was more rueful than anything. "Don't tell me Ridge doesn't feel the same way sometimes. I think he, more than any of us, has found it hard to embrace the whole Fortune existence."

"I don't think it's *embracing* the Fortunes as much as it is turning his back on being a Windham," she said, then wondered if she was telling Sabrina something she shouldn't.

"Yeah." Her expression pinched. "Our father's cancer

progressed so fast. We barely knew about it before he was summarily selling the company and we were trying to find something suitable to wear for the funeral."

"I'm sorry. It must have been very painful."

"We all deal with loss in our own way." Sabrina looked almost as if she wanted to say more, but she suddenly pointed. "Office supplies!" she said with deliberate brightness, aiming the cart out of the baby section and making a beeline for the school and home office displays. She snatched up a package of bright yellow pencils. "I go through these faster than you can imagine."

Hope smiled, content enough to follow Sabrina's lead away from the depressing subject as well as her surprisingly aimless progress around the giant discount department store. Even though it was Saturday, Ridge was working, so it wasn't as if Hope had needed to be home for him.

Her cheeks warmed, thinking about the night before. The kisses on the deck.

She feared he regretted kissing her altogether. *I'm sorry,* he'd said. *I shouldn't have.* He'd been pushing her away even before she'd realized Evie had awakened.

What else was that to mean? She wasn't entirely oblivious. She *knew* he'd wanted her as much as she wanted him. She'd felt the proof.

But even if she'd had the nerve, it wasn't as if she could've asked him. He'd been closed up on his side of the house when she'd finally ventured out again once Evie was asleep—something that had taken almost two unbearably long hours. After hovering in the great room, feeling torn between the desire to boldly cross to his side of the house and confront the matter head-on, and the cowardice of leaving sleeping dogs alone, cowardice had won out.

She'd spent a nearly sleepless night tormenting herself

over every word spoken and every breath shared, only to sleep long past his departure from the house that morning, aided considerably by the fact that Evie had also awoken later than usual.

Ridge's only communication had been the note he'd left in his slashing handwriting that he'd be working all day.

So when Sabrina unexpectedly called her for advice, Hope had pounced on the opportunity like a gift from above. She would have agreed to nearly anything just to avoid the way he was obviously avoiding *her*.

"Let's go to lunch," Sabrina said once she aimed her cart through the checkout. "Or are you in a hurry to get back to that precious Evie of yours?"

Wendy had been periodically sending Hope snapshots of herself and the baby. To be honest, Hope wasn't sure which one of them looked like they were having more fun.

"I'm not usually away from her for more than an hour or two at a time…but we could have lunch," she agreed faintly. Sabrina was something of a force and it was hard not to get swept along. Particularly when the woman tucked her arm through Hope's as if they were the best of girlfriends.

"Excellent! I know the cutest place at the shopping center next to the FortuneMetals complex." Sabrina laughed as they started across the busy parking lot. "Wonder if Cousin Reeve is there?" She wrinkled her nose, looking surprisingly mischievous. "Have you heard of him? Reeve Fortune?"

Hope lifted her shoulders. "Erm—"

Sabrina laughed again. "The surname notwithstanding," she said drolly, "he's a big-time overachiever. Runs Fortune-Metals *and* FortuneMedia."

Hope's eyebrows rose. "I've heard of FortuneMedia at least." One of the business offices in Chatelaine near the Daily Grind, in fact, had a big FortuneMedia sign on it. Considering the building used to be an old house, the sign had always struck her as too modern. "Isn't that the company that keeps buying up smaller media outlets?"

"So I've heard. Bought up the company that produces *The Chatelaine Report*. Have you seen it?"

Hope shook her head.

"It's a community event blog. We've been promoting the petting zoo on it for the last month. Anyway, Reeve ended up marrying the woman who used to write it, Isabel Banninger. Was apparently all the scandal around here a year or two ago. She was engaged to Trey Fitzgerald and made it all the way to the church but ran out on him 'cause his cheating was caught all over the internet. You've *surely* heard of the Fitzgeralds? Daddy is big-time into politics?"

Hope tapped her forehead. "Sorry. If I have, I've forgotten."

Sabrina gasped and pressed her hand to her mouth. "God! How insensitive I am." She looked so genuinely distressed that Hope would have done a backflip to ease the moment.

"It's fine," she insisted. "Some things I *do* remember. And some things I don't. That's just the way it is." It sounded so much easier to deal with than it really was, but she loathed the idea that people who knew felt sorry for her because of it.

"Well, I just can't imagine it." Sabrina beeped the doors of her vehicle as they approached it, and the liftgate automatically opened. "But I think you're handling it amazingly well."

"I'm only handling it because Ridge insists on taking care of everything." The words came out before she could stop them, and she felt her face flush. "I'll get all this." She quickly reached for one of the overloaded bags. "You already look like you're ready to pop."

For a second, she thought Sabrina was going to argue. But Ridge's sister's smile widened ruefully. "Yeah, I feel like I'm about ready to sometimes, too." She blew out her breath, rubbing her back as she moved to the driver's side and hauled herself up behind the steering wheel.

Hope quickly transferred the purchases into the back of the SUV. She looked up at the opened liftgate above her head. Even if she jumped, she didn't think she'd reach the button to close it. "Can you close it from up there?"

"Sure thing."

Hope ducked out of the way when the wide door began descending again, and waited until she heard the secure sound of it locking into place before she climbed up into the passenger seat. "Does your OB think you'll make it to your due date?"

"Hopefully, but we're keeping close track. One scare to the hospital was enough for Zane and me." Rather than backing out of the parking spot, though, Sabrina sat there for a moment, tapping the steering wheel with her thumb. "He's like that, you know," she said quietly.

Hope's mouth dried a little. Sabrina wasn't referring to either her obstetrician or fiancé, but to Ridge. "Generous to a fault?"

"That. But also, he's a fixer by nature."

Hope looked down at her clenched hands in her lap. "I don't like knowing I need fixing."

Sabrina's hand immediately reached over and covered Hope's. "Not *you*," she said firmly. She squeezed her hand in emphasis. "Fixing your situation."

"But I should be doing more for myself," she said huskily. She looked up at the other woman. "Shouldn't I?"

Sabrina's brows twitched together for a moment as she placed her hands on the steering wheel again. She was obviously taking Hope's words to heart. "Like what? You mean like getting a job?"

She lifted her shoulders. "Maybe? I can't imagine who'd hire me, though. I can't even say whether I have a college education. What kind of experience I have." She made a face. "If any."

"Well, I'd hire you in a second," Sabrina said so matter-of-factly that Hope believed her. She started backing out of the parking spot. "Regardless of what you remember about yourself, you're honest, conscientious and motivated. I can't tell you how many people I've met who have a basketful of degrees yet possess none of those attributes. I'll take one employee who is interested in learning and showing up over five who aren't. If we had a spot at all in the ranch office, I'd tell you it's yours."

"I wasn't asking—"

"I know you weren't," Sabrina assured just as swiftly. "If you could choose to be anything at all—without regard to education or experience or any of that—what would it be?"

"A good mom," Hope said immediately.

Sabrina pressed her hand to her swollen belly. "Amen to that." Then she gave Hope a quick wink. "I know it's probably annoying to hear but have patience. Things will unfold in time. I'm certain of it."

How many times had Ridge told her something similar?

"Patience is overrated," she muttered and then huffed out a deep sigh.

Sabrina smiled at her. And Hope smiled back.

As they continued driving through the streets of Corpus Christi, Hope peered through the windows, wondering if she'd spot anything that might be familiar.

As far as she knew, none of the yearbooks came from a Central High School located there.

"Talking about patience, though, I have to admit I wouldn't

mind being a few weeks early," Sabrina said suddenly. "Nothing crazy of course, but how *huge* am I going to get?"

Hope laughed. "I was enormous." She pressed her hands against her belly, looking down at herself, and so easily picturing her abdomen. "It was like having an alien living inside me, watching Evie moving around inside that huge belly!"

"Try having two of 'em," Sabrina said feelingly.

Hope's mind immediately took a detour into the land of make-believe. Twins obviously ran in Ridge's family. When he had a baby—

Her phone pinged with another picture from Wendy, and Hope managed to get her mind off of Ridge making babies.

She flashed the picture of Evie and Wendy grinning into the camera at Sabrina when she stopped at a light.

"I think they're having more fun without us," Sabrina chuckled.

Hope smiled, too, and saved the picture to that great, mysterious thing called the cloud. She already had hundreds of pictures filling up her cloud. The cell phone was yet one more thing that Ridge had provided for her as well as an email account and that metaphorical puffy white storage space.

Whatever the future held, at least she'd have the photos she'd taken. The phone might need to be left behind, but that email account and all of its trappings were forever hers.

When she and Sabrina were seated in the cute little café, which overlooked the park next to the FortuneMetals skyscraper, and had ordered, Sabrina pulled a notepad out of her purse and spread it on the table. She flipped a few pages, all of which were covered with lists of one sort or another.

"What *is* all that?"

"Lists," Sabrina stated the obvious. "In the last month I can't seem to stop making them. I'm afraid I'm becoming obsessed, actually. This one—" she flipped to one page that was covered with neat handwriting and wildly color-ful checkmarks "—is an inventory of all the bed linens we have!" She shook her head at herself and turned to another page. "Honestly, I don't know how Zane stands it."

Hope grinned. "Because he adores you," she said. "Lists and all."

Sabrina was flipping more pages, murmuring slightly to herself. "Thank God," she replied. She pulled out a pencil and busily marked off items under a large heading of NURS-ERY, then she turned another page and sat back slightly. "The wedding."

Hope was doctoring the iced tea the waitress delivered. She knew Sabrina and Zane were thinking sometime after the babies were born, and a part of her couldn't help wonder-ing if she and Evie would still be there to see it.

The knot twisting in her stomach was becoming much too familiar.

"Have you set a date, then?" she asked a little desperately.

"Not yet." Fortunately, Sabrina noticed nothing amiss as she tapped her page with the eraser end of the pencil. "This is about the mystery wedding." She sat forward, lowering her voice confidingly. "I think I've figured out who is get-ting married."

Hope raised her eyebrows, surprised. "Really! How? And who?"

"Process of elimination."

Hope waited. "And?"

Sabrina sat back to let the waitress place their orders on the table. As soon as she was gone again, Sabrina leaned forward again. "Belinda and Javier."

Hope blinked, taking a fraction of a second to place the names. "Belinda Mendes?"

Sabrina was nodding. "And Javier Mendes."

"Aren't they already married?" The middle-aged couple were longstanding employees at the ranch. They even lived in one of the bungalows near the ranch headquarters. Hope walked past it every time she and Evie went to the petting zoo. Belinda's flower garden was a treat almost as sweet as the zoo.

"Married *and* divorced. Three times. And from what I hear, they're overdue to remarry." Sabrina picked up one of the wedges of her sliced club sandwich. "And it would make sense why we've all been invited."

"But why not just let everyone know it's them?"

"Who knows?" Sabrina waved her hand, and a little slice of tomato slid out of her sandwich and landed on the plate. "Hedging their bets? Less embarrassment if they cancel out altogether before the big day?" She took a quick bite before her gesturing lost even more bits of sandwich ingredients. "And I bet you that my *mother* knows the truth. Which is why she is making sure that we all attend."

Hope thought it was a bit of a stretch, but who was she to judge? "I guess it makes about as much sense as anything else."

"Well, I'm pretty sure I'm right," Sabrina said, looking satisfied with her conclusion. "Wish they would've just done it a month ago, though. I've grown out of the dress I was planning to wear." She shook her head. "Won't fasten over the boobal region anymore." She patted her cleavage.

Hope couldn't help but laugh. Yes, Sabrina was *very* pregnant with an impressive watermelon-sized baby bump and a bosom to match. "I'm sure you'll find something that works."

"Easy for you to say, Miss Size Two."

Hope gave a snort of laughter. "Not even in my dreams anymore. When I was in high school, I was a zero." She didn't really know where the knowledge came from. Like the other memories, it just seemed to be *there*. As if it had never been missing in the first place.

"You're killing me." Sabrina pulled a comical face. "A zero. Good grief. Now, the least you can do is help me find a dress, too."

Hope started to shake her head again. She knew how close Sabrina was to her sisters. Surely, they'd be better at the dress matter. "I—"

"There's a boutique right here in the complex," Sabrina interjected. "DD's Designs. We could pop in after we finish here. The owner's a friend of mine from a women-in-business association." She seemed to realize she was still holding a pencil in one hand and her sandwich in the other and stuck the pencil behind her ear.

"A maternity boutique?" Hope immediately envisioned something as chic as Lullababies.

"Not exactly maternity clothes. But if I could find something flowy enough maybe I could get by without having to visit Ollie the Tent Maker."

"You hardly need a *tent*."

"Perhaps not. But we're here." Sabrina gestured toward the windows that lined one wall of the fancy little café. "And I hate wasting a good opportunity."

Hope wavered. She glanced at her phone again.

Her companion noticed. "My mother and Evie will be fine for an extra few minutes," she promised.

"I know, but I don't want to take advantage of—"

Sabrina let out a laugh. "Seriously? Nobody takes advantage of my mother. She'd make mincemeat out of them without turning a single blond hair and smile graciously right through the bloodletting."

"Now I *know* you're exaggerating." Wendy Fortune was the epitome of classy elegance, even when she was mugging for a selfie in the company of an eight-month-old. "Blood-letting?"

"Might be a slight exaggeration," Sabrina allowed. She reached over and squeezed Hope's hand. "Come on. How often do we get a chance to indulge ourselves with just some girl time?"

She made it sound so appealing that Hope found herself capitulating even before she'd made the conscious decision to do so. "But just the one shop, right? I really *don't* want to be away from Evie too much longer."

"Well, when you put it like that…" Sabrina winked. "One shop." She gestured at their plates. Her sandwich was half-eaten already whereas Hope had barely taken a single bite of hers. "So get cracking there, girlfriend. Eating is fine. But it has got nothing on shopping for clothes, and you have a baby to get back to."

Two hours later and driving up the ranch road once more, Hope knew she'd never doubt Ridge's sister when her mind was set on something.

Not only had Sabrina found herself a lovely dress to wear to the "sshh, Mendes wedding," but she'd gotten two other casual outfits for herself, one for her twin, Dahlia, and when that hadn't proved fulfilling enough, she'd insisted on turning her focus on Hope.

Which is why Hope had stored three shopping bags in the back seat of the SUV and not two.

"I'll pay you back," Hope said for about the fifth time since Sabrina had insisted that the watercolor silk dress was positively made for Hope.

"Whenever," she said with the careless ease that only someone who has never worried about money could carry off. "You heard Deedee yourself when she rang it up. Friends and family discount she said."

In the great blankness of her past, Hope was certain that she would never have paid such an extravagant amount for a dress, no matter how beautiful. If it weren't for that discount— nearly 75 percent off the full price—she would have certainly been able to resist Sabrina's well-intentioned coaxing to buy the thing. "Well, as a friend of her friend, thank you."

"Wait until Ridge sees you in it. You'll knock him speechless."

Hope pressed her tongue against the back of her teeth, trying and failing to suppress a little shiver. Regardless of his reaction, though, she no longer had an excuse to avoid attending the Mendeses' mystery wedding. Because whether or not he regretted kissing her, she didn't doubt for one second that he wouldn't hesitate to use her as an excuse not to go himself if she refused.

She didn't want that on her conscience, too.

Her gaze lingered on the headquarter buildings as Sabrina drove past them. "You really think it's Belinda and Javier, huh?"

"Pretty positive. Dahlia, Jade and I started a pool to see who's right. Not that I should admit to having insider knowledge, but Belinda and Javier both requested vacation beginning the day before the wedding. Perfect timing for a honeymoon. That's what clinched it for me, anyway. It's just too coincidental to ignore, don't you think?"

It did seem like a reasonable conclusion to Hope. She cordoned off the part of her mind that was intent on conjuring details of a ceremony that had culminated in a wedding ring on *her* finger and prayed that her fractured mind wasn't visible on the outside. "Who do Dahlia and Jade think the couple is?"

"Dahlia's betting on Dr. Mitch and his office manager, Alondra. Jade's undecided."

"*My* Dr. Mitch?"

"If Dahlia's right, he's Alondra's Dr. Mitch," Sabrina said humorously. "Pump my brother on it. If I'm backing the wrong horse, I want to know. It'll keep me from losing any money on Belinda and Javier!"

Hope tried not to choke. The idea of "pumping" Ridge for anything was too disturbing. But somehow, she managed to produce a chuckle in response.

Sabrina's steady stream of chatter fortunately didn't require a lot of input, and it wasn't long before she dropped Hope off at Wendy's house.

Ridge's SUV, which she had used that morning when she'd met up with his sister, was still parked where she'd left it.

Sabrina hung her head out the window after Hope had her shopping bag in hand. "Tell Mom I'd have stopped in, but I'm dying to get out of these pants, and I'll see her tomorrow for brunch!" Then she waved and drove off.

Hope headed toward the beautiful house, the shopping bag from DD's Designs swinging from her hand. Before she could even ring the doorbell, though, the door swung open to reveal Wendy's smiling face. She was a tall, slender woman with enviably sleek blond hair cut in a flattering bob and striking green eyes.

"Come in, darling. I didn't even hear you drive up. I was just showing these gentlemen out." Wendy wrapped her arm through Hope's and pulled her right into the house, stepping aside while several of the ranch hands trooped out—Javier Mendes among them. They all tipped their hats politely as they departed. "Just had to discuss a little ranch business." She shut the door after them. "Now, tell me all about your day. Did Sabrina wear you out?"

"No...not entirely." She felt a quick jab of self-consciousness when she heard more male voices from inside the house and recognized Ridge's right away. Sighing, she pushed her fingers self-consciously through her hair. She'd had the window partially down for part of the drive, and her hair was probably a mess. "She said she'd see you tomorrow for brunch."

"I've talked all of my children into brunch at The Chef's Table," she said. "You and Evie included, of course."

Hope knew the fancy restaurant was located at the LC Club and opened her mouth to demur, but they'd just entered the great room and she spotted Ridge standing next to the enormous stone fireplace.

He was holding Evie, who was, not surprisingly, giving him the usual looks of adoration. Ridge, however, was looking at Hope, and she felt a kaleidoscope of butterflies suddenly take flight inside her. It was a wonder she didn't sprout wings herself and flutter her way right on over to him. Her lips even tingled, as if it was only moments ago that his lips had been pressed against them rather than the better part of an entire day.

Mercifully, Wendy's arm around Hope's kept her grounded while she doggedly recalled Ridge's *I'm sorry, I shouldn't have* and peripherally noticed Arlo and Nash were also present. Whatever ranch business it was had been important enough to call them all together on a Saturday afternoon.

"I was just telling everyone how much I enjoyed watching Evie today," Wendy was saying. "She's an absolute joy. Brings me right back to when my little ones were little."

"Mom's in the mood for reminiscing," Arlo deadpanned. Like all of Wendy's offspring, Arlo was tall. But where Ridge and Nash both were dark-haired and dark-eyed, Arlo was blond like Sabrina and Dahlia. "Next thing she'll be telling us who had diaper rash and who didn't."

Wendy reached out and cradled Arlo's cheek in her palm. "I could recall who was the one most likely to run out of the house stark naked," she said with a fond tap as his cheek turned a little ruddy.

"Busted," Nash drawled. He was leaning on the enormous kitchen island, a squat glass of something amber held in his long fingers. "I dearly hope it's a habit you've finally outgrown."

Arlo raised his eyebrows. "At least I never got poison oak on the parts the sun's not supposed to see like *someone* I know."

"Oh, my. Nash really was truly miserable," Wendy said. "Easy to laugh about now."

"Easy for you to say," Nash grumbled. "I was eight and the memory still pains me."

"And this one—" Wendy let go of Hope and poked Ridge in the center of his chest "—had to be watched every minute of the day, too."

Ridge shook his head, but his mother just laughed and moved across the room to where an array of cut crystal bottles were arranged on a tray. She eschewed the liquor, though, for a bottle of water. "He was forever trying to fix things."

Hope set her shopping bag on a side table. Some things didn't change, she thought.

Wendy threw herself down in the corner of the oversize leather couch, leisurely crossing her long legs. "I had an antique table in my dressing room," she said. "And my youngest there—" she tilted the bottom of her bottle in Ridge's direction "—decided the legs were an inch too long. So, with his toy toolbox full of *supposedly* toy tools, he cut exactly an inch off each leg." Her sparkling gaze focused on Hope. "He was five," she added. "My advice to you is to never allow Evie to own a toy toolbox no matter how harmless the tools appear to be."

"Five!" Hope didn't have to work hard to imagine a little boy with waving brown hair, inquisitive brown eyes and an unexpectedly mischievous grin. "And you had an actual saw?"

"Didn't need a saw." Ridge shrugged. "I used the hammer and the screwdriver like a wedge."

"And sanded it all when he was done with my set of vintage steel nail files," Wendy finished.

"The table legs were about two inches in diameter," Ridge retorted. "It wasn't as though I was cutting chunks of wood like the legs on that." He moved Evie to his other arm and gestured carelessly at the solidly framed coffee table in front of the couch.

"By the time he was eight, he'd moved on from redesigning furniture to blowing up stuff," Nash said.

Hope raised her eyebrows. *"Stuff?"*

"I liked experimenting," Ridge said dismissively. "And not all mints dropped into a bottle of soda react like the old Mentos in soda trick."

"There were times I think you liked the *mess*," Wendy said wryly. "Particularly when it ended up dripping down from the ceiling."

"Well. Speaking of messes…" Hope bent and gathered up Evie's scattered toys. "I hope Evie didn't make too much of one." She straightened and stuffed them in the diaper bag that sat on the other end of the couch.

"I look forward to many messes with that little one," Wendy assured.

As if cleaning up the toys were a signal, both Arlo and Nash began making their exits. They kissed Wendy's cheek, bumped Ridge's fist, tousled Evie's hair and tipped nonexistent Stetsons toward Hope as they left.

All perfectly normal behavior.

But Hope still felt a faint frisson of unease that had nothing to do with Ridge and a moonlit lake and whether or not he regretted kissing her.

It wasn't unusual for his siblings to gather together for no reason at all. They were a close family.

And her being a worrywart was starting to spill over onto too many unrelated matters.

Focus. Just focus on one thing. Take a breath and let everything else go.

She exhaled slowly as she shouldered the diaper bag and held out her arms for the one thing that never failed. Evie. The pale skin around her daughter's eyes was looking pink— a sure sign that she was getting sleepy. "I should get her down for a nap. Any later and it'll be impossible to get her to sleep tonight at a reasonable hour."

"I'll come with you." Ridge transferred the baby to her. "I rode with Arlo earlier."

Hope nodded and snuggled Evie's neck, inhaling the sweet baby scent for a long, needy moment before she looked at Wendy once more. "Thank you ag—"

The older woman cut her off with a languid wave. "Enough thanks, my dear. She's a delight, and I'll be begging you soon enough for a repeat." She stood and picked up Hope's shopping bag, peeking through the tissue paper that poked artfully out the top of it. "What lovely colors," she murmured.

"I needed a dress for the M—" She almost said Mendes but corrected hurriedly with, "mystery wedding."

If anything, Wendy looked even more pleased. She tilted her cheek to accept Ridge's light kiss before they all headed into the foyer. Then his mom pulled open the door and handed Ridge the shopping bag. "Don't forget brunch tomorrow."

"How can we? You've put reminders on all of our calendars," he told her.

"A mother learns these things," she said blithely, and

watched them until they reached Ridge's SUV before she went inside and closed the door again.

Hope fastened Evie into her car seat and hoped she wouldn't fall asleep on the short drive to his place. If she did, she'd probably figure the five minutes would be enough of a nap to last her, and Hope knew from experience that would mean a very cranky Evie come nighttime.

She climbed into the passenger seat and took the shopping bag that Ridge handed over to her. The tissue paper crinkled softly as she set it near her feet and fastened her seat belt.

"So." She folded her hands in her lap and looked at him. "Is it my imagination or—" she swirled her index finger in the air "—have you all been circling the wagons?"

Chapter Eight

Timing, Ridge thought, was everything.

It was impossible to ignore the inquisitive, vaguely imperious expression on Hope's face. It reminded him, strangely enough, of the way his mom could look sometimes when she knew something was off.

If she'd have arrived just five minutes later, everyone would have already been gone from Wendy's house and Hope would have never known a thing about the impromptu meeting Nash had called after one of the hands reported seeing that suspicious car again.

"It's—" fully prepared to lie, it aggravated the life out of him that he couldn't "—not your imagination." The gravel spun a little under his tires as he accelerated down his mother's drive toward the gate.

He could sense Hope's muscles tensing, though her expression didn't change.

"A gray sedan was seen on the access road that runs back behind Dahlia's place," he admitted. "One of the hands reported it to Nash. Everyone on the ranch has been told to keep an eye out for it."

Her lips compressed slightly. She nodded and turned forward. Her profile was sharply outlined by the deepening afternoon sun. "When?"

"When were they told or when did they see it?"

Her eyebrow lifted slightly. "Is this why Sabrina took me out of town today?"

"What?" He felt his neck get hot. "No. The car wasn't spotted until you'd already left. It was around noon today." While he'd been on the other side of Chatelaine, traipsing around the Zazlo place with Beau Weatherly.

She sucked in a breath. Exhaled even more slowly.

Then she shifted and crossed her arms over her chest.

The bag near her feet crinkled.

What would Hope think of the property? The house was half the size of the one they occupied now.

He cleared his throat. It was always too easy for his thoughts to get ahead of himself where she was concerned. "Since Nash saw the car the first time, he spread the word to keep watch. After you saw it in town, we've emphasized it to everyone. The good news, though, is this time we got a partial license plate."

Surprise softened her stiff posture, and she looked at him again. "How partial?"

"First three numbers. But it's a Nebraska license plate. I got the information to Villanueva. Nash also has someone with the sheriff's department working on the number. The focus is narrowing."

"Nebraska…" she murmured.

His hands felt sweaty around the steering wheel, and he lowered his window all the way down. "Does it feel familiar?"

She was looking out the side window. The wind from his window stirred her hair. She made a soft sound as she shook her head.

Ridge glanced in the rearview mirror. Thanks to the mirror that hung on the back seat to reflect the baby's rear-facing car seat, he could see Evie's head bobbing. Nearly asleep but determined to stave it off.

How could he bear to lose either one of them?

He cleared his throat yet again. "Meanwhile, I think it's time we started using the gate at the end of the drive."

She gave him a look. "You're *that* worried?"

"Cautious," he corrected. "Everyone is going to be using their gates. It's already been agreed upon. We'll stop again when…" He shrugged. "When we have all this figured out," he finally concluded.

"Great. I'm inconveniencing everyone now."

"You're not inconveniencing anyone. I told you…we're all on the same page." He drummed the steering wheel with his thumb a few times. "How, uh, how was Corpus? Sabrina leave anything on the shelves for someone else to buy? Figure she's going to have a baby shower at some point. Is there anything left to get her?"

"She didn't buy a lot of diapers," Hope said. "Diapers are always a good shower gift." She was quiet for a moment. Then tucked her drifting hair behind her ear.

He'd spent an inordinate amount of time studying her ears. Along with every other little detail about her.

She had pierced ears. But had never worn any earrings. Did she dislike them? Was she allergic?

The key pendant he'd gotten her was platinum and diamond.

Sabrina told him that lots of people had sensitivities to jewelry but not usually platinum.

"Diapers." His thumb drummed the steering wheel. Why wouldn't Hope wear the damn necklace? "I'll have to remember that."

Her hand fluttered to the paper twine handles of the shopping bag. "I bought a dress," she said.

His neck got a few degrees hotter. Short of turning on the air conditioning in fifty-degree weather or sticking his head outside the open window like a dog, he had to live with it. "Yeah?"

"For the, um, the wedding."

As if he didn't know that.

"Sabrina loaned me the money," she added a little pedantically. "I intend to pay her back."

He was pretty certain that Sabrina didn't worry about getting repaid. He also thought he showed good sense not mentioning that, however. "Great. That's great."

"It's not from GreatStore."

"I don't care where it's from. As long as you feel good about it and don't leave me to fend for myself at the thing."

She faced him once more, arms crossed again. "Aren't you the least bit curious who is getting married? Your sisters have started a pool on it, you know."

He didn't, but even if he did, he just did not care. He spread his fingers away from the steering wheel. "I have the feeling that an honest answer is going to get me into hot water."

She made a sound and shook her head. "Men," she murmured.

He managed not to smile, but it was an effort. "I have it on good authority from my mother that we're an impossible lot." He glanced in the rearview mirror again. "We're not going to make it before she's asleep."

She craned her head around to look back at her daughter's reflection in the specialized mirror. "Thirty minutes," she said. "If she just could sleep for thirty minutes, then we'll all sleep better tonight."

They'd reached the closed gate for his turnoff. He drove right past it.

"Where are we going?"

"Anywhere. So long as it takes at least thirty minutes."

"I *knew* she kept you awake at night, too."

Yeah. It was *Evie* who kept him awake at all hours.

He just smiled wryly and kept driving.

They made it all the way around the entire lake. They drove by the Fortune Castle, where only one tradesman truck was still parked outside. His mother's renovations of the place to turn it into a boutique hotel were nearly complete.

He'd seen it only a few times before she'd started the mammoth undertaking. From what he could see, the outside had changed little, except the moat of unruly bushes that had surrounded the property had been eradicated and new landscaping installed in its place.

He knew better than to stop entirely, though. It was the constant motion that kept Evie sleeping soundly. Instead, he trolled past the unlikely structure, while Hope made admiring sounds about the blooming sunset behind the turrets.

When they hit the thirty-minute mark, he looked at Hope. Her head was resting against the seatback, her eyes at half-mast as she watched the sky. She was almost as relaxed as Evie. One hand resting on the console between them. The other hand occasionally pulling her hair away from her face.

It was all he could do not to pull over and reach for her. Kiss her all over again, even if it did mean waking up the most effective eight-month-old chaperone who'd ever existed. "Keep going or head home?"

"Keep going." Her gaze slanted toward him. Periwinkle blue at dusk. "Only if you don't mind…"

If it meant a few more minutes between now and the reality of returned memories, he'd drive forever.

Instead of turning back toward the lake, he drove instead toward the town of Chatelaine.

The air blowing through the window was getting chillier, but she wasn't complaining, so he left it alone. "Haven't taken you to Harv's New BBQ yet, have I?"

She shook her head. Brushed her hair back from her face again and gave him a sideways look. "What happened to Harv's Old BBQ?"

"Who knows? Guess you'd have to ask Harv."

She smiled slightly, then turned her palm upward against the console between them. "Maybe I will."

He'd been kicking himself for kissing her the other night. Not because he regretted it. Kissing her had been a long time in coming. But he felt like a man dying of thirst who'd been given the faintest taste of water. It only worsened the wanting.

None of which stopped him from settling his hand lightly atop her palm. And why something so simple could feel so freaking erotic, he had no idea. But he was glad the wind blowing through his window was on the verge of cold.

He was pretty sure she'd wonder why he'd suddenly stick his head out the window otherwise.

"Ridge?"

Heat was streaking down his spine. "Yeah."

She hesitated, and he moved his hand away, so he wouldn't have to endure her doing it first.

"Last night. I'm sorry about—" her fingers curled into a small fist, though her hand remained on the console "—about throwing myself at, uh, at you—"

His head whipped around. There was still plenty of light to see her cheeks had turned red. "What are you talking about?"

"On the deck. I kissed—"

"*I* kissed you," he said over her. He closed his hand over her fist. "And the only thing *I'm sorry* about is moving too fast for you."

"*That's* what you regret?"

"Who said anything about regret?" He realized he'd tightened his hand around her fist and deliberately lightened his grip.

"You. You said you were sorry, you shouldn't have—"

He checked the road and pulled abruptly off onto the shoulder, kicking up a cloud of dust. He shoved the gear to Park and turned to look at her. "I *shouldn't* have rushed you," he said flatly. "I'm not sure what would have happened if Evie hadn't started crying when she did."

Hope's face looked even rosier. "Would that have been so terrible?"

The desire that was a constant simmer inside him went straight to boil. "You're the one who is doubting your own memories about your husband's funeral. Are you married? Not married?"

She sucked in an audible breath. "I don't feel married."

"Right now? Or period?"

She didn't answer and his head felt too heavy. He closed his eyes and ground his teeth for a short millennium. He felt her shifting and looked at her again. She was staring at her palms in her lap.

Imagining a band on her wedding finger, no doubt.

He reached over and deliberately covered her left hand again with his. "I don't want to be something *you* regret, Hope. Not now. Not later." His voice sounded as raw as the words felt.

"Why did you call me that?"

The question threw him. "Call you what? Hope?"

"You're the one who gave me the name in the first place. Why Hope?"

"Should I have stuck with *Hey You*?" He immediately regretted the sarcasm. "Because it was the first thing that came to me," he said. "I looked at you and I thought—" his jaw felt tight "—I *felt* Hope."

His admission seemed to echo around them.

Then her palm shifted, pressing up against his, molding them together. Her fingers slid slightly, gliding through his fingers.

If the way her palm curled against his was any indication of how other elements would fit, he could die a happy man.

But only if he could be certain she didn't belong to someone else.

"I don't want to be something you regret, either," she said softly.

Honk!

They both startled, sitting back in their seats when the semitrailer blew past their SUV, leaving it rocking in its wake.

"Jerk," Hope muttered.

Ridge had a stronger word for the honking driver, who had also woken Evie.

Hope unfastened her seat belt and leaned over into the back seat, getting the baby situated again with the pacifier. Then she slid back into her own seat beside him. She fastened her seat belt. "We agree, then." Her voice was soft but steadfastly calm. "We don't want to do something we'll regret."

That hadn't strictly been what either one of them had said, but just as he was set to gnaw on it, she shook back her hair and lifted her chin slightly. "Doesn't stop us from being friends. And friends—" she moistened her lips "—can hold hands." She set her hand on the console again in an unmistakable invitation. "Right?"

His blood pounded in his ears. Nothing about Hope would ever be *just friends*.

He shifted into Drive, threaded his fingers through hers

and steered back onto the road with his other hand. "Right."
Some lies were meant to be forgiven.

For a small-town Saturday night, Harv's New BBQ was
hopping.

He dropped Hope and Evie off in front of the restaurant
since the crammed parking lot meant he had to park down
the block. When he joined them, they were in line with another dozen people after them.

No table service was available at Harv's. You waited your
turn to order at the counter, carried your own food to one of
the many picnic tables lined up outside the place and cleared
your own mess away when you were done.

Big propane heaters were scattered among the tables, casting enough heat that you didn't really feel the cold. String
lights bobbed lightly overhead, suspended in a long criss-
cross pattern between the Harv's rooftop to the tall poles that
separated the perimeter from the used tire place next door.

They sat across from each other, shoulder and hip against
complete strangers who were just as neck-deep as they were
in some of the best BBQ that Ridge had ever tasted. A three-
piece band was wedged into the only speck of covered patio
that existed. The enthusiasm in their music definitely superseded their talent, but nobody seemed to mind. There were as
many people two-stepping between the tables as were eating.

A young couple one table over had a little boy. Definitely
older than Evie, but between the food that Hope cut up for
her and the entertaining faces the child was making at her,
she was as happy as a piglet in clover.

Ridge went back to stand in that godforsaken long line,
after they'd stuffed themselves to the gills with brisket and
pulled pork and hot sausages, just to buy a wedge of chocolate cream pie topped with half a foot of whipped cream.
And knew he'd do it twenty times over, just to see Hope's

face wreathed in laughter at the way Evie wanted to dive into the stuff.

Then the three of them did their own share of two-stepping, only to lose their seats at the picnic table to usurpers who were just as neck-deep in their own food.

Hope took Evie into the restroom and returned with a considerably less sticky baby. He scooped her daughter into his arms, and they walked, hand in hand, the two blocks back to the Escalade while she raved about Harv's food, and he wondered what she'd think of Nonny Zazlo's spread only another ten minutes or so straight up the road.

Then she spotted his SUV. "For heaven's sake," she exclaimed. "What's wrong with people?"

"Hunger for Harv's, I guess." Two ancient pickups had parked so close he was nearly blocked in. He almost wished they had because it would have delayed the end of their evening. But thanks to the technology on his SUV, he could have maneuvered his way out of nearly anything, and while she and Evie waited off to one side, now was no exception.

He pulled abreast of the first pickup. It had a cracked windshield, a bench seat patterned in fraying plaid and a flag hanging from a pole mounted in the truck bed.

Hope fastened Evie into her seat and climbed into her own. "There is no way that guy could have parked any closer to you."

"Not without making baby trucks."

She fastened her seat belt and jabbed the button for her heated seat. "I hadn't realized how cold it was getting."

He'd take credit for that fact if it wasn't for all those propane heaters.

Unlike the crowded Harv's, the main drag of Chatelaine was quiet, and moments later, he pulled out in a U-turn and aimed toward the lake.

"It's been a good day." Hope broke the silence when they were halfway home.

"Yeah." And he would have traded his fancy-ass SUV for a pickup truck with a cracked windshield in a hot second, just to have that bench seat, so—*friends* be damned—he could put his arm around her and pull her close to his side. He'd keep her there for as long as he could.

Timing. It was everything.

And Nebraska—and whatever was lurking there—was getting closer by the minute.

The next morning, Hope was getting Evie buckled into her car seat when Gordon Villanueva called Ridge.

They were already running late to meet his family at The Chef's Table for brunch, but Ridge stepped away from the SUV to take the call. "What've you got," he greeted.

Some people would be offended by the lack of niceties. Villanueva wasn't one of them. "We've narrowed down the vehicles to six. Two are rental cars. Four privately owned. I'm emailing you the list of full plates. Meanwhile, I'm headed to Nebraska in a few hours. Want to see the registered owners in person."

"You're not telling them what you're—"

"Cool your jets, son," Villanueva said mildly. "I'm seeking information. Not planning to dole it out."

Ridge's shoulders came down again. He smoothed the tails of his necktie. He'd worn one only a handful of times since moving to Chatelaine Hills, but The Chef's Table called for a certain amount of formality. "Sorry," he muttered.

"No need to apologize. It's a stressful situation for y'all. Anyways, I should have more news for you by the end of the day, even if it is just to say there's no connection at all."

"Thanks," Ridge said, but Villanueva had already ended the call.

He pocketed his cell phone and walked back to the vehicle.

Hope was already sitting in the passenger seat. She was wearing skinny black jeans tucked into knee-high boots and a bright blue turtleneck that she'd gotten from one of his sisters for Christmas. The color made her eyes look even bluer.

"That was Gordon Villanueva." He climbed in beside her and conveyed the latest. He turned the engine over and put the SUV in gear. It wouldn't take long to get to the LC Club, but they were still going to be nearly a half hour late. His fault for losing track of time that morning when he'd gone down to the barn early to work with Larry, Moe and Curly.

"So, we might know who I am by tonight." Her voice was as tight as the pinched line that had formed between her eyebrows.

"We might know who *the driver* of that car is," he corrected. "It's a piece of the puzzle, but it doesn't necessarily mean we'll have a direct line pointing to your real identity."

"I wish Hope *was* my real identity," she muttered.

"Once you know the truth, you'll feel differently."

"Will I?"

It was a question that he was wholly unequipped to answer, and they both knew it.

He slowed as he neared the gate, waiting for it to slowly swing open when he hit the switch. But it only swung a few feet before it ground to a halt.

"Sit tight." He got out and checked the mechanism that powered the heavy steel. After making a few adjustments, he got the gate going again, and soon they were speeding along the ranch road. It was nearly eleven thirty in the morning. The sun was shining, and there was a faint breeze causing ripples on the lake. As they drove around the lake, he saw at least a half dozen small sailboats out to take advantage of the day.

He envied them a little. Most of his experience with boats was of the luxury yacht variety.

"I left a phone message at Mitch's office this morning," she said when they'd finally reached the farthest point of the lake and turned onto the main drag, which wound between the cluster of businesses and the shoreline walk that was busy with joggers and skateboarders. "Asking for a recommendation for a therapist."

He stopped at a crosswalk, and while they waited for a woman pushing a stroller to cross, he looked from Hope to the sandy beach that stretched from the walk to the glittering water. A kid ran in the sand while trying to get his red kite aloft.

Had Ridge ever looked that carefree?

Felt that carefree?

The roadway cleared, and he hit the gas again and glanced at Hope. "I could have just called Mitch directly."

"I know you could have." She crossed one slender leg over the other. The toe of her boot bobbed up and down. "But I need to start doing more for myself." She shoveled her lustrous hair away from her face. "Can't expect you to take care of everything forever."

Why not?

He didn't voice the words, knowing how antiquated he'd sound if he did, but he meant them all the same.

What was wrong with a man who wanted to take care of those he lo—

A low-slung sports car suddenly shot out of a side road right in front of them, and Ridge jammed the brakes, automatically throwing his arm out in front of Hope, who'd pitched forward despite her seat belt. He glared at the departing license plate—TFIII. "You okay?"

"Fine." She sounded breathless. "Um—"

He belatedly realized the arm he'd thrown in front of her had landed squarely over her breasts. One of which fit oh-so-neatly in the cup of his palm.

He rapidly moved his hand away. "Sorry."

But he wasn't.

Not even a little.

Chapter Nine

The LC Club was a sprawling multistory building of cascading terraces and balconies topped with red slate tiles that sat right on the shore of Lake Chatelaine, and on that day, one entire terrace level of The Chef's Table—just one of the designated restaurants at the LC Club—was occupied by Ridge's family.

The wall of windows that were opened when the weather was warm were currently closed, but that didn't hinder the spectacular view of the seemingly endless lake.

The brunch that Wendy had arranged might have sounded simple when his mother talked about it, but the lavish buffet that had been set up for them was anything but. She could take the Windham out of her name, but some things where Wendy Fortune was concerned didn't change. Entertaining in style—even if the guests were just her family—was one of them.

"She's very good with children," his mother said.

She was sitting beside Ridge in the easy chairs situated closest to the windows. On the enclosed terrace several feet below their window, Hope had command of both Evie and Colt, as well as little two-year-old Aviva, who was being raised by Arlo's fiancée, Carrie. Their terrace fed right out onto the beach, though the windows were also currently closed, and they had it all to themselves. Which meant the colorful beach ball that Aviva was chasing endlessly didn't bother a single other soul.

For most of the time since they'd arrived at the restaurant, Hope had seemed to deliberately occupy herself with someone *other* than Ridge. The fact that those others happened to all be miniature people was moot.

"She is." He watched Hope lightly bop the beach ball so it landed perfectly enough that Aviva could catch it. The toddler's squealing laughter penetrated the windows separating them. "Hope's good with people, period."

His mom made a soft little *mmm* sound.

"So, what really spurred this brunch thing?" He swept his arm behind him. Sabrina and Dahlia were heads together at one table, leaving their fiancés to the football game playing out on an oversize television. Nash and Imani were ensconced together on a love seat as if they'd gotten stuck together by glue, and Arlo and Carrie were still picking at the array of bite-size desserts set on a multitiered glass display.

"Not a single thing," she said so airily he didn't believe her for a second.

He scooped a tiny spoonful of caviar from the tin and dabbed it on a crème-fraîche-topped blin. Nobody else had been eating the blini so he'd commandeered the whole dang tray of them, as well as the crystal bowl of ice holding the caviar tin. "Are you sick?"

She frowned at him. "Whatever makes you ask a question like that?"

Gauche or not, he folded the small blin in half and ate the entire thing in one bite. When he'd swallowed, he wiped his mouth with a napkin that he tossed atop the remaining morsels. He'd already eaten so many of them he was stuffed.

"That time that Dad scheduled a family dinner." Tried to, anyway, since nobody had agreed to go.

Only after the fact did Ridge realize that was probably about the time that Casper knew he was dying.

His mother's complexion lost a little color. "Oh, honey," she sighed. Then shook her head slightly and tucked her hair behind one ear. She reached over, squeezing his hand. "I've never been healthier." Her cheeks regained their usual color. "Or, for that matter, happier. But time does move swiftly. All of you—" her nod took in the others behind them "—are on the cusp of the most wonderful life changes, and I want to savor it all."

"Mom," he chided in a low tone. "You begged, cajoled and pretty much bribed us with *cabins*—" he accompanied the mocking term for their lavish lakeside homes with air quotes "—to move to Chatelaine Hills. We see each other nearly every day."

"You don't have to analyze everything in life, Ridge. Sometimes you can just enjoy for the sake of enjoying."

His gaze drifted out the window again. Below, Hope was holding Colt on her lap while Aviva, apparently disinterested now in the beach ball, played with Hope's long hair and Evie crawled over her legs. "Enjoying with no concern for consequences is a little dangerous, don't you think?"

"Honey, my entire life has been about the consequences. Consequences for my own choices when I was younger than you are now. Consequences of the choices made by parents I never even knew. Choices by your father, by Wendell Fortune. The list goes on and on…"

"You're making my point."

"Ridge." Her tone held a gentle reprimand. "My point is you can't *always* worry about consequences. Things happen in our lives over which we have absolutely no control.

If you're not careful, happiness can slip through your fingers like sand in the wind. You couldn't have changed your father's choice to sell Windham Plastics even if he'd given us all some notice about it."

"Why'd you stay with him?" Ridge suddenly pinned his gaze on her. "Seriously. Why?"

She blinked slowly. "When I married Casper—said those vows—I was head over heels in love with him. All of you were conceived in love, Ridge. I know you don't believe it but it's true. I thought I'd married my knight in shining armor. He'd wed the poor little Texas beauty pageant trophy winner and turned her into his queen. And our fantasies lasted, until they didn't. But we'd still said those vows."

"But you weren't happy."

"Neither was he," Wendy said gently.

"I don't see how he suddenly has your understanding."

She smiled faintly. "It's not all that sudden. I'm sad for the handsome knight who became too blind and callous to appreciate the family he'd had right under his nose."

"But not sad enough to keep his name."

Her gaze softened even more. Typically, she was reading his thoughts before he could even articulate them. "If I'd divorced him, do you think I would have kept my married name?" Her gaze went to the rafters.

He hadn't inherited her ability to read minds and he wondered what thoughts were in hers.

"You'd have gone back to being Wendy Wilson," he concluded.

"Ah." She lifted her index finger. "But even that wasn't accurate, was it? My real mother's surname was McQueen. If she hadn't been illegitimate, it would have been Fortune." She spread both palms, and the collection of diamond bracelets on her slender wrist sent prisms dancing. "And here we are."

"Embracing all things Fortune," he muttered.

"You know that I appreciate the…loyalty…you all showed by taking the name. But if you're happier still being Windham, I would understand."

"Maybe you take understanding too far, Mom. Instead of brunches with *us*, you should be looking for something for yourself. You've still got a few good years left—"

She snorted inelegantly. "Oh, Ridge. Thank you *so* much for *that*."

"You know what I mean."

She just laughed good-naturedly and pushed herself out of the deeply cushioned chair. The lines of her narrow fitting ivory suit fell perfectly into place. "I've said it before, and I'll say it again. When I'm interested in changing the current state of my love life, I'll be sure to let you know. Until then, save all the suggestions and leave me in peace. Trust me." Her smile took on a mocking tilt. "I am doing perfectly *fine*." She picked up the napkin-covered plate of blini and carried it over to the buffet table, where Carrie was laughingly trying to finger-feed a bite of something to Arlo, who was steadfastly shaking his head.

However, Ridge's attention wasn't on his siblings or their partners.

It was on Hope.

And a partial Nebraska license plate number.

"Hey." Jade nudged the elbow he'd propped on the arm of his chair and snickered when he jerked. "Heath and I are going to do one of the Chatelaine mine tours and take a little hike. He picked up a map from the Chatelaine museum last week, and it has all the old, abandoned mines marked on it. You and Hope want to come along? Everyone else has already bowed out. Don't you do it, too."

"I wouldn't suggest holding your breath. I doubt Hope'll want to leave Evie for two afternoons running."

His sister raised her eyebrows. "Maybe *ask* her what she wants to do rather than assume?"

Ridge grumbled under his breath. Save him from women who always thought they knew better than him.

"Fine." He pushed to his feet. "I'll ask her. But I'm telling you…" He went out the swinging glass door that was barely distinguishable from the windows that surrounded it.

His assessment had been spot on.

Hope did *not* want to leave Evie for another afternoon. "Can't we take her with us?" she asked instead. "She loves being outside and never minds the carrier."

He wanted to traipse around the countryside looking at boarded-up mines about as much as he wanted a hole drilled in his head. But he also wasn't inclined to disappoint Hope. So, he nodded, and they all agreed to meet up again a little later after they'd had a chance to change into more suitable clothes.

When they did reconvene on the other side of Chatelaine, it was at a dusty spot marked with a big sign that proclaimed Joyride Silver Mine Tour!

While Jade and Heath purchased tickets for the four of them, Hope slathered baby-safe sunblock all over Evie, tied a flowery-patterned bonnet on her silky auburn head and deftly maneuvered her into the baby carrier. Now that her daughter was getting so much bigger, she could position the carrier either in front of her or in back.

That afternoon, she chose the back. "She's gaining weight," Hope said. "It's getting easier to carry her this way."

"I could carry her," Ridge offered. He wasn't sure why he hadn't thought of it before.

But she was shaking her head. "I don't think the carrier would fit you."

Considering Hope was no bigger than a minute and he topped her by a foot, he didn't bother arguing.

Jade was holding up the colorful brochure that contained the map of the other mines nearby. She'd marked a route on it in yellow highlighter. "Here's your copy," she told him. "Just in case we get separated after we're done with the tour here."

Ridge glanced at the map and was more than a little disconcerted to realize one of the stops colored in yellow was squarely within the Zazlo property. He also noticed there was no mention in the brochure or on the map of the silver mine Wendell Fortune and his brother had owned. Before its deadly collapse, it had been the most profitable mine around. "Surprised the Fortune Mine isn't listed despite the way it ended."

Heath reached out and tapped a spot on the map some distance farther out from town. "It was around there. The museum where I picked up the brochures has a whole display."

"Have you always had an interest in abandoned mines?" Ridge asked as he tucked a bottle of water in the mesh side pocket of Evie's carrier for Hope.

"Only since I'm marrying the great-granddaughter of a mine owner," Heath replied humorously. He leaned over and kissed Jade's nose. She positively glowed as she beamed back at him.

Ridge sincerely hoped they didn't plan to be all lovey-dovey the entire afternoon. It was his sister, after all.

And judging by the vaguely goading glint in her eyes as she slid a look his way, Jade knew exactly how he felt.

"Tour in two minutes!" An ancient-looking old man with a beard that could have housed a flock of birds stood in the doorway of a modest-looking rustic building. "Don't matter if you got tickets or not. You're late, you're out of the tour. No refunds." He stomped back inside.

"Friendly guy," Hope said under her breath.

Stuffing an extra bottle of water inside one of the cargo pockets of his pants, Ridge silently agreed.

They all filed through the narrow doorway into the building, which turned out to be a gift shop selling a myriad variety of snacks and cold drinks, jewelry, and simple toys like jacks and bouncing balls and not-so-simple things like hand-carved slingshots.

While they waited for the second hand to tick down the last minute, Ridge glanced in one of the glass jewelry displays. It held dozens of silver rings. Some with stones. Others without.

"Afternoon." He smiled at the old woman guarding the case, and she preened a little, plumping up her gray hair that was so wild it needed no plumping whatsoever.

"Afternoon," she returned and tapped the glass case with a gnarled finger. "Silver in these rings comes from this very mine," she said. "Artisan crafted and all." She smiled broadly, showing off a missing molar and creating dozens more wrinkly intersections on an already lined face. "They make a fine wedding band." Her gaze went tellingly toward Hope, who blushed and hurried over to the elderly man who had pulled a hardhat fitted with a light on the front down from a peg.

He plunked the hat on his head. "I'm Harv," he yelled so abruptly that Hope nearly jumped back a foot. "I'm your tour guide here at the Joyride. And don't be asking for discount coupons for my goodfernuthin' grandson's bar-bee-cue down the road." If the derision in his voice weren't apparent enough, the sneer curling one corner of his lip put a magnifying glass on it. "Boy's got no family loyalty." He turned and pushed at a rough-hewn section of wall behind him, and it slid back to reveal a yawning cavern with a set of steps going down into the darkness. "Don't see *him* sending folks my way, do you?"

Hope's round gaze sought Ridge's as if to ask *are we sure we want to do this?*

Suddenly, he forgot about wondering what sort of wedding ring Hope had remembered wearing and found himself stepping closer to her. He gently nudged Evie's hat in place where it had slid to one side. Her eyes were nearly closed, but she still held fast to her crinkly fabric book.

Jade and Heath followed Harv down the steps, quickly disappearing into the gloom. The old man's voice echoed back up to them.

"Mind your heads," he warned. "Them wood beams go back more 'n a hunnert 'n thirty years when the Joyride was first established in 1894."

The gray-haired woman handed Ridge a sturdy flashlight before he passed through the opening after Hope and Evie.

He flipped it on and directed the strong beam down the steps. While he'd never considered himself claustrophobic, those steps seemed to go down forever.

Hope had hesitated a few steps down from him, and she looked back up at him. Anticipation lit her features as brightly as his flashlight did the steps under their feet. "Come on," she said, beckoning with her hand. "They're going to get too far ahead of us."

"Wouldn't matter," he said wryly and ducked his head to avoid hitting the first of the series of beams that held the earth at bay as they descended. "Could hear old Harv from a mile away."

The old codger's voice was booming back to them, recounting the trials and triumphs of mining through the ages, and by the time Ridge and Hope reached the bottom of the stairs and the tunnel widened out, he'd gotten sucked into the tales just like the others. He brought up the rear, the beam of his flashlight bouncing around the pathway and walls despite the ancient lanterns that were spaced out along the way. Whether intentional or not, the bulbs flickered intermittently.

The lure of silver, copper, gold and whatever else they were finding down in these depths that had ensnared his great-grandfather, Wendell Fortune, and his brothers hadn't transmitted down through the genes to Ridge, that was for sure.

Only by looking at his cell phone was he able to tell how long they'd been walking when they finally stopped in a large, mostly square room crammed with ancient wooden crates, coiled ropes, bed rolls and tools gone red with rust. Ridge could feel a draft of cool, fresh air, and imagined what it would have felt like when there'd been no ventilation pipes hiding in the dusty corners.

He pulled the water bottle from his pocket and took a long drink. He, for one, was grateful for modern conveniences. He was also glad that Evie was sound asleep.

No future bad dreams for her, at least.

Heath and Jade were roving around the room, peering at this, asking questions about that. Telling ol' Harv that their great-granddaddy had been none other than Wendell Fortune.

Hope, however, edged closer to Ridge. "You alright?" she whispered.

"Swell." He guzzled another quarter of his water bottle.

The flickering lantern lights sent shadows dancing over their faces, but Ridge could still see the curve of her soft lips.

She leaned even closer. "We're almost through," she whispered.

"How do you know?" Harv's tales were interesting, but the man sounded as though he could go on forever.

"Tour lasts an hour," she said. "It's more than half over now."

If his cell phone was to be trusted, more like 70 percent over now.

Thirty percent to go. He could stand that.

Particularly when Hope slid her hand through his arm and stood so close to him. Probably just because of that cold air coming through the pipes, but he wasn't going to look a gift horse in the mouth.

"O' course, you don't need me to tell you about the Fortune Mine collapse." Harv's booming voice was only slightly toned down in the room. He hitched one skinny hip up on the corner of a slatted crate, which held a facsimile of bags of flour alongside at least a dozen sticks of dynamite.

Ridge hoped they were fakes, at least.

"Mining's always been a dangerous pursuit," Harv said. "But all them folks dyin'…" He tsked and shook his head dolefully. "Tragic is what it was."

A tragedy that had lived on even longer thanks to the years of deceits and secrets maintained not just by Wendell and his brothers but by their future generations.

Seemed like Casper Windham had been truer to that nature than Wendy. He'd only seemed to find more caring for his fellow humanity when he'd learned he'd been dying. Only last month had Arlo shared his discovery that Casper had paid for the cancer treatments of everyone else who'd been in the hospital at the same time he'd been there. That he'd made sure that all of the patients' kids had toys at Christmastime.

"Did you lose family or friends in the mine collapse?" Jade asked Harv.

The old man shook his head. "No family. A couple of friends, though. The Joy here—" he hopped back to his feet, surprisingly spry, and clapped his hand around a support beam "—was competing against the Fortune Mining Company. Much as she could, anyway. The Fortunes were always a lucky bunch of cusses." His face screwed up for a minute. "Beggin' pardon, to ya'll. Don't mean to offend."

In his odd, rolling gait, he started out of the room again, switching on the headlamp on his helmet as he went.

As far as safety gear went, if it was actually necessary, he ought to have handed out hard hats to all of them.

Once again, Ridge looked beyond the obvious trappings and started to see the nearly invisible signs of modern day. He was an engineer, after all. He could appreciate ingenuity.

The Joyride Silver Mine tour might look like it was still living in the early 1900s. But it was all for show.

And he'd gotten sucked into it as much as anyone else.

Even having figured that out, though, he still breathed more easily after they reached the top of the earthen steps and Harv pushed the mock wall back in place.

"Hope you enjoyed the tour," he said. "Appreciate you tellin' your friends about us if you did." Harv offered a squinty smile at them. "And if you didn't, appreciate you keepin' that all to yourself."

Heath pushed a wadded bill into the jar sitting next to the whisky barrel that apparently doubled as a seat for Harv when he wasn't conducting business. A hand-printed sign above the jar said TIPS. "We did enjoy it," he assured the old man, reaching out to shake his hand. "Very informative. Thank you."

"Glad to share." Harv tapped his temple with his index finger. "Worst thing a man can do is go to his grave hoarding stuff up here."

Hope turned away from Harv before he could see her expression tighten, but Ridge saw it and knew she was thinking about the memories that *her* mind was currently hoarding.

He added his own tip to the jar and followed her out into the sunshine, where she was loosening the straps of her carrier and deftly maneuvering Evie around so that she was facing Hope.

"Want to call it a day?" he asked her. There was still the hike that Jade had mapped out that included the abandoned mine on the Zazlo spread.

"Not at all," Hope said quickly. She cradled Evie's padded rear through the carrier, huffing a little as she tried to re-configure the straps for the new position.

"Here." Ridge wrapped his hands around the upper straps, taking Evie's weight off of Hope long enough that she could complete the task. And somehow, by the time she was successful, they were standing as close together as two people could stand, considering the eight-month Evie right between them. "Better?"

Hope's throat worked. She moistened her lips, her gaze landing on his and flitting away again. Pink color rode her cheekbones. "You, um, you can let go of the straps now," she whispered.

His knuckles were pressed against her flesh. If he stretched out his fingers, they'd brush her breasts. He cleared his throat and let go of the straps. Jade and Heath had exited the gift shop and were coming their way. "Gonna refill my water bottle," Ridge said and turned in the other direction.

The last thing he needed just then was Jade and her hawk-like attention noticing he was more in need of a dunk under cold water than he was a paltry drink of it.

Chapter Ten

"Look." More than an hour later, two pit stops to change and feed Evie, who'd woken up, and a lazy debate with Jade, who'd decided to go one way when they reached a fork in the trail while Ridge wanted to go the other, Hope stopped in the middle of the shrubby field they were walking. "That's a farmhouse. We *are* on private property." She shaded her eyes with one hand and propped the other on her hip, slowly turning in a circle. "Did we lose the trail you think?"

Ridge shook his head. He'd shed his sweatshirt before they'd left the Joyride and wished that he could shed his shirt, too. He contented himself with adding another roll to his rolled-up sleeves. As far as he was concerned, it wasn't supposed to be this warm in January. "We didn't lose the trail," he assured.

Her brilliant blue gaze turned his way. "How do you know?"

"This is the Zazlo ranch," he said. "We crossed onto it when we passed the water tower a while back. Nonny Zazlo died last year. Has no relatives to inherit it."

"Surprised Zane Baston hasn't bought it up." She said the same thing that Ridge had. She turned in a circle again and automatically caught the crinkle book when Evie tossed it at her head. "I guess that means nobody's living in that cute farmhouse." She sent a grin toward Ridge. "At least I don't feel so bad trespassing now."

He suddenly felt as inept as a teenager with a crush on the untouchable homecoming queen. "You think it's cute?"

"Big old covered porch and all those shutters? It's like something Joanna Gaines would design. Who *wouldn't* love it?"

He didn't know who Joanna Gaines was, but he didn't care. "I'm thinking about buying it," he admitted even though he hadn't intended on admitting any such thing.

Her jaw dropped slightly, and her cheeks paled. "You want to move?" Her lashes swept down suddenly. "C-congratulations." She looked down at Evie, crinkling the book even more as she lightly tapped her daughter on the head with it, and the baby babbled nonsensically as she took the book from her mother and then shoved one corner in her mouth.

Full of crinkly fabric book or not didn't stop Evie from chattering away.

Hope retied the baby's hat under her chin and pulled out the water bottle from the mesh side pocket. She flipped the pull top, squirted water into her mouth, then Evie's, then sent a small stream of it down the back of her shirt before she tucked it back in the pocket. "Awfully warm for January." She briskly set off in the direction they'd been walking. "How much further to the mine?"

She'd already pushed up the long sleeves of her T-shirt. Now the wet fabric clung to her spine before disappearing under the waist of her faded blue jeans. As she quickly picked her way over and around sage-green clumps of scrubby grass, Ridge couldn't keep his attention off the sway of her hips.

"Not far," he answered belatedly. He didn't have to pull the map out of his pocket to know that. The mine was near the northern border, which he knew was marked by a shelterbelt of trees that ran perpendicular to the creek that marked the eastern border. "And I haven't decided for sure about moving."

She lifted one hand, obviously using it to keep her balance as she stepped over a decaying log. He caught up to her, prepared to help.

"I've got it," she said a little testily.

He turned up his palm.

"And of course you want to move," she added, still cranky. "Everyone wants something they can call their own. Dahlia has her sheep, Jade the petting zoo. Nash runs the show. Sabrina writes the checks. Arlo already had his own business, and you—"

"Fill in the gaps," he said shortly.

"I was going to say that you had Windham Plastics until it was taken away."

"Good to know I'm an open book," he muttered.

"Don't expect me to feel sorry for you," she said tartly. "You can buy anything you want." She waved her hand in the general direction of the farmhouse that had already fallen far behind them thanks to the new clip in her step. "Including Zaney Nazlo's place."

"Nonny Zazlo," he murmured.

She flapped her hand. "Whatever. Ranch. Don't ranch. Invent another gizmo. Your choices are endless." She snatched her water bottle again and took a drink, her pace never slowing. "How soon?"

"Before I decide?"

"Before you move."

He was starting to feel testy himself. "Hard to say when I'm not sure if I want it bad enough to break my mom's heart."

"Your mother practically worships the ground you walk on. She's like that with all of you. She's not going to stop just because you decide to leave the nest."

He grimaced. "I left the *nest* when I was twenty."

"Bully for you. At least you had a nest. I didn't even have—" She stopped abruptly, and this time when Evie tossed her crinkle book, it sailed right beyond her mama's shoulder.

Ridge scooped it up and caught up to Hope. "What?"

She just shook her head a little, pinching her eyes closed. "I didn't have parents," she said thickly. "I grew up in foster homes. Group homes."

He stifled an oath and started to reach for her, but she shook her head. "Don't."

He curled his fingers into fists. "Hope."

"If you touch me right now, I'm going to start crying, which will only upset Evie." She didn't look at him. "All I remember were group homes. No specific foster parents."

"Anything before the group homes?" If she'd lost her parents as a young child or a baby even, surely she would have had an actual foster family. He didn't know a lot about it, but group homes were designed for older kids. Weren't they?

"No." Her voice was so brittle, it hurt to hear it. "So just, just tell me where the stupid *mine* is so at least I can say it's something I've achieved."

He swallowed a dozen questions that didn't want to be swallowed.

"We keep walking until we reach those trees." He pointed toward the horizon where the tops of the trees were just becoming visible. The land sloped downward toward them, so the distance was deceiving.

She nodded silently and set off once more.

Where were the foster homes?

Did she remember any other names?

"I think the last group home was called something like Goldstone." Her voice floated back at him, uncannily responding to the questions pounding inside his head. "I remember going on a ski trip to Gatlinburg. On a bus. I think it took an entire day getting there."

He just managed not to pull out his cell phone to start calculating how many places were a day's bus ride away from Gatlinburg, Tennessee. "Do you remember how old you were?"

"No. Yes." Her footsteps paused. "Thirteen." She waited a beat. Then repeated it with more certainty. "Thirteen. I had a friend. She was sixteen. Amy Smith. She wanted her driver's license *bad*. That ski trip was the most fun we'd ever had," she said finally, and started walking again.

It was a treasure trove of information.

He quickly thumbed the details into a text and sent it off to Villanueva, fortunately managing not to trip over his feet from not watching where he was going as he followed her.

They crested the gentle hill and descended into the valley on the other side. The mine was marked only by a boarded entrance bearing a heavy latch that was chained and locked.

Hope walked over and crouched down on one knee in front of it. A faded placard was nailed into the wood. "Fester Mine," she read. "The images *that* evokes are lovely. I thought it was just called Mine 32."

"Mine 32 is what the map says. Maybe Fester was someone's name."

"Rough name. Fester like an untreated wound. Of course, my real name could be equally as awful."

He didn't know why, when it was so important to find out her real name, it was a relief that she hadn't remembered it along with the details about living in foster care. "It won't be awful."

"When it turns out to be Gangreenia Crudbucket I'll remind you of that." She pushed to her feet and rattled the chain and lock.

He was glad to see that both were in good shape. They'd obviously been replaced fairly recently. Beau Weatherly hadn't mentioned the mine, which made him wonder if the other man even knew of its location on the property. It was only a minor curiosity. Weatherly couldn't *really* know everything, though there were times that it felt like it. "Gangreenia?"

She lifted her shoulder. "Live without knowing your own name a while," she said. "You'd come up with dozens of possibilities, too. I must admit I prefer the name Hope."

He wrapped his arms around her and Evie. Felt Hope's stiff resistance for only a few seconds before it drained away and she gave an exhausted sounding sigh.

"Did Amy get her driver's license?"

She shook her head. "Nobody willing to sign the paperwork for her." Her forehead fell to his chest. "She ran away a few months after that ski trip. Never saw her again. I don't think I made a lot of friends after her," she added quietly.

He pressed his cheek to hers, holding her even closer until Evie squawked a protest over being squashed between them.

Hope's eyes looked drier than his felt. "Ready to go home?" he asked.

"Ready to go back." She gave a twisted smile that held no humor. "But it seems like it's not really home. Not for either one of us."

She jiggled Evie and shook her head a few times. "Enough depressing myself," she said determinedly and once again set off in the direction they'd come.

When they passed the empty farmhouse again, she waved her arm, encompassing. "Totally Joanna," she pronounced. But after that, it was only Evie who kept up a running litany of ga-ga-gas and ba-ba-bas.

Jade and Heath were already waiting when they reached the spot off the highway where they'd left their vehicles. The two of them were sitting next to each other on the opened tailgate of Heath's truck.

"Find Number 32?" Jade hopped off the tailgate when Hope blew out a long breath and began detaching Evie and the carrier.

"Yeah." Ridge thought it was pretty noble of him not to point out that the buttons on Jade's shirt were buttoned all wrong. "Aka the Fester Mine. You find yours?"

"Um, no." His sister shook her head. "It was so hot, and we found this sweet little lake that was all shady, so we hung out there for a while instead."

"Mmm." Explained the misaligned buttons.

He lifted the back hatch of the SUV, and Hope set Evie in the cargo area while she dug in the diaper bag for a change of clothes. Evie's clothes were as damp from sweat as Hope's were.

"Thought we'd stop at the Saddle and Spur," Heath said. "Grab an early dinner."

"Steak with a side of steak," Jade quipped.

Ridge knew without having to ask that more socializing was the last thing Hope wanted to do. "It's been a busy day for Evie," he said.

Jade nodded. Her gaze was busy moving between him and Hope. At least *they* didn't have mismatched buttons.

At the rate they were going, would they ever?

Jade and Heath departed, and Ridge got behind the wheel and started up the engine and the air-conditioning while Hope finished up with Evie.

Not for the first time, he checked his cell phone for some response from Villanueva, but there was none.

He knew the investigator would check in at some point. He always did, even if the report was only that there was nothing new *to* report.

"Know what it's like to be waiting for answers," he'd said when Ridge had first hired him. Now, while trying to distract himself from everything in his life that felt undone and unfinished, Ridge wondered what unanswered questions had tormented Villanueva.

He also wondered what the odds were that one of the registered owners the investigator was planning to meet had been involved in foster care.

Then Hope opened the passenger door and climbed up beside him and sent his thoughts scattering. He realized she'd fastened Evie—now dressed in a plain white T-shirt and a diaper—into her car seat already.

They drove back through Chatelaine. The town seemed even sleepier than usual on a Sunday evening. Only a few other vehicles besides Heath's were parked next to the Saddle and Spur. They left the town behind, and with no traffic to speak of, soon reached the lake.

He stopped long enough to pick up pizza from Shoreline Pizza, and then turned toward Chatelaine Hills. The aroma of the pizza had his stomach growling by the time they finally turned through the gate, which this time opened and closed right on command.

After parking along the side of the house, they went in through the back door.

Hope settled Evie in her high chair with a squeezable food pouch and a handful of cereal puffs. "Can you watch her for a few minutes while I change?"

In answer, he pulled out the bar stool next to Evie, and Hope practically jogged out of the room.

He stole one of Evie's tasteless cereal puffs. "Do you know who Joanna Gaines is?"

She smiled toothily at him and pitched her food pouch over the side of her high chair. He picked it off the floor, wiped the squeeze top and gave it back to her. But when she went to throw it again, he pulled it out of her reach. "Ah, no. I'm on to your games, princess."

Evie swept her hand across the tray, scattering as many puffs as she caught, which she lifted to her mouth and shoved inside with all the busy diligence of a squirrel readying for winter.

He got up and retrieved her sippy cup, filling it with water, and set it nearby. Then he sat back down and flipped back the pizza box lid.

The pie inside was still hot, the melting cheese bearing just the right amount of overdone brownness and the pepperonis curling crisply around the edges. He started to lift out a piece when his phone chirped.

He dropped the piece back onto the cardboard box and picked up his cell phone.

Villanueva.

His hand felt strangely unsteady. He ran his other hand over the baby's head. "What're we hoping for here, Evie?"

She opened her smiling mouth to show him the puffs she was still munching.

He leaned over and kissed her forehead. "You keep me sane, baby girl."

He straightened again and thumbed open the message.

No luck in Nebraska. None of the auto owners have an apparent connection to Hope. Will verify but don't expect to find they weren't all on the up and up. Good details about foster care. Tennessee is a long way from Nebraska. Will dig further.

Ridge closed the message and turned his phone face down on the counter.

He picked up the pizza again.

He'd eaten two pieces and successfully fed Evie half the food pouch when Hope returned, freshly showered and dressed in a loose-fitting gray T-shirt dress that reached all the way down to her bare toes.

She took the bar stool across from him and folded her hands together atop the counter. "I think it's time for Evie and me to move out."

"No." He pushed the box of pizza toward her. He'd saved his crusts for her.

Her lips compressed for a moment. But he could see her eyeing the crusts.

They were her favorite part.

Not the cheese. Not the toppings.

Just the crusty edge.

It could be doughy. It could be browned and nearly burnt to a crisp. Didn't matter. She ate them regardless, as if they were a delicacy.

He took a third slice for himself, starting at the pointed end like any sane person did.

She shifted on the bar stool, as if she was trying to make herself physically taller. "I really think it'd be best if—"

"No," he mumbled around the pizza in his mouth. He swallowed. Got up to retrieve an IPA from the fridge for himself and a bottle of cola for her. He sat again and picked up the slice once more.

"I'd rather have a beer," she said and returned the cola to the fridge. She set the IPA deliberately in front of him and twisted off the cap.

He watched her over the pizza, wondering how long it'd be before she caved. She liked beer even less than she liked strong coffee.

She took a swift sip, tried and failed to hide the resulting grimace, then chased it down with a huge bite of pizza crust.

She lifted her chin a little. "Just because you say *no*—" she growled out the word in a deep tone that he assumed was meant to mimic him "—doesn't mean I have to listen."

"Where would you go?"

Her brilliant eyes darkened almost to navy. "There's a shelter in—"

"Definitely no. I don't care *where* it is." He pushed aside the box and clasped her hands, beer bottle and all, between his. "Why the sudden urge to abandon me?" He tried, yet failed, to keep his voice light. Easy.

"Well, *you're* going to move."

Realization dawned. His sisters had accused him more than once of being obtuse. Now he had to wonder if they'd had a point. "*If* I move, and that—" her mouth opened, and he spoke over her "—is a big if, of course you and Evie would come with me."

Her eyebrows pulled together. "You need to stop feeling responsible for us, Ridge. Just because you found us in your barn—"

"I don't feel responsible for you." A bigger lie didn't exist. "I want you both with me." The raw truth of that part balanced things out. "I've gotten used to you."

"Like what? A pair of slippers?" She rolled her eyes.

"Don't knock a good pair of slippers." He released her hands and picked up his pizza again. "If it's so important to you, though, you could use the guesthouse."

She stared. "What?"

He'd considered the idea before—inspired by Nash, who'd done that very thing with Imani only a few months ago. But Hope had seemed content to be right where she was. With him. And he had no interest at all in changing that.

But he had enough smarts to know that standing in her way wasn't the right thing to do, either. And if she was in his guesthouse, she'd be closer than some *shelter* in Godknows-where, where he'd have no chance of protecting her at all from whatever—or whomever—lurked in her past.

"It's not much more than a studio setup," he warned. "No real proper bedroom and just a kitchenette." But there was a full bathroom and some ancient furniture the previous owners had left. "The kitchen in the house is always open for you to use, of course."

He'd have had to be sightless to miss the sudden light in Hope's eyes. The way her entire body seemed to lean forward with interest. "But what about you and the Nazlo farmhouse?"

"Zazlo."

"Whatever."

"Even if it works out, if I decide I *want* it to work out, it'll take time. It's not the only place to consider."

Her eyes widened. "Y-you're looking at more than one place?"

"Well, so far I've only seen—" He shook his head. They were getting off track. "The point is nothing is imminent."

"Where else, though?"

He was starting to feel a little harried. "Oklahoma."

Her mouth rounded. "That's…a bit further."

Understatement of the year. "It's just a thought. The place doesn't even have a ranch house because it burned down."

"Oh, well, then you have to go with Fester Mine's house."

"Nonny Zazlo," he said crisply. "That house needs some renovations—"

"Not too many, I hope." Her cheeks flushed. "I mean, it looked charming from the outside at least."

Exasperation was building. The topic wasn't about his

problems. It was about hers. "Do you want to use the guest-house or don't you?"

She pressed her lips together for a moment. Then nodded, which was at least one thing he'd fully expected.

"Yes, please," she said fervently.

"It's still full of crap from my place in Dallas." A small mountain of stuff that he hadn't decided to part with but also hadn't had room for in the fully furnished house from his mother. "It'll take a day or two to clean it out."

"I don't care." She hopped off her bar stool and darted around the island, throwing her arms around his neck. "Thank you." She pressed her lips against his cheek.

His hand automatically went to the small of her back. She smelled like morning rain and midnight desire.

"Didn't know you were that anxious to leave."

She pulled back only slightly. "I'm *not* anxious to leave." She barely waited a breath. "When can we start cleaning it out?"

Given that he was voluntarily putting space between them, it was odd that he couldn't suppress a sudden laugh. Even if it did feel as rusty as the tools down in the Joyride Silver Mine. "Next week?"

"Perfect." She kissed his cheek again and then practically danced over to Evie, who had sucked down most of the contents of the pouch and was only half-covered in the rest, and lifted her free of the high chair. Hope held her high above her head and laughed up into her baby's face. "Guess what you and Mommy are going to do?"

He pushed aside the pizza and reached for his beer.

Ridge knew exactly what Evie and her mommy were going to do.

Break his heart.

Chapter Eleven

"And what about *this*?"

Dahlia's tone was waspish, and Ridge looked over at his sister. It was Monday morning, and she was the only one who'd volunteered some time to help him deal with the mess of items he'd more or less dumped into the guesthouse last summer. "It's my polo gear," he told her.

"You haven't played polo in years."

"So?"

She rolled her eyes and tossed the bulging sport bag out of the closet that she'd been mining. The bag landed atop the pile of similar bags, teetered a little and started to slide down the side. "So why did you bother bringing it here?" She pushed her hair back from her face and stretched her back. "Along with the boxing gloves and the tennis rackets and the fencing gear?"

He turned back to the stack of packing boxes that he hadn't had the sense to label and now, all these months later, didn't have a clue what they contained. "Because I didn't take the time in Dallas to clean out. Obviously." He sliced through the packing tape and flipped open the cardboard flaps.

Ski boots.

A wad of T-shirts that he'd had since college.

A wooden crate from Mendoza Winery.

No wonder the box was so heavy. It was full of booze and boots.

Last time he'd used the boots was in Gstaad. He'd gone there after earning his most recent master's degree. For a while, he'd been an avid skier. But he'd never gone to Gatlinburg, Tennessee.

The boots didn't interest him, but the wine was another story, and he lifted the crate out of the box. The dozen bottles of wine it contained had been packed by the winery in millions of pieces of crinkled cardboard that scattered over the floor as soon as he extracted one of the bottles. Merlot. "I forgot all about the wine."

"Think you forgot all about a lot of stuff," Dahlia muttered. "I had no idea you were such a pack rat, Ridge."

"Not even close to a pack rat," he said absently. The bottle was slightly dusty from the packing material. He rubbed his thumb over the foiled label, polishing. "Dad sent me the case when we got the patent approved on T349."

His sister stopped next to him. Dahlia's relationship with their father, on the surface at least, hadn't been as fractious as some of theirs. "The case is still full. You never drank any of it?"

He shook his head. He remembered how surprised he'd been reading the card that came with the wine. Written by Casper himself, rather than by his secretary.

Ridge hefted the crate out of the way of the mess of packing materials and packing boxes. He made room for it on the crowded granite breakfast bar and then turned back to survey the progress they'd made.

He'd begun clearing things out after Hope and Evie had left for their daily trek down to Jade's petting zoo. Ridge had finally learned to keep his trap closed when it came to Hope's insistence on walking, even though there were per-

fectly good golf carts around that would have made short
work of the distance. And that morning, he'd been glad of
her choices, because it meant he could estimate pretty well
the amount of time he had before she'd return.

While he'd hoped to surprise her by having the place
cleared out by then, he hadn't counted on the breadth of the
task until he'd actually gone inside the guesthouse for the
first time since moving there.

"I'm gonna pull the truck around," he told Dahlia. "Toss
everything in the back that'll fit and drop it at the donation
center in Chatelaine." He blew out his breath. "It should only
take me about five trips," he muttered.

"I realize it sounds odd when I've been complaining for
the last hour, but are you sure you want to give it *all* away?"

"I'm sure. Get rid of everything. Except this." He thumped
his hand on the wooden wine crate. "So, if you want something we've already unpacked, now's your chance."

She immediately reached for one of the sport bags.

"You and Rawlston taking up disc golf?"

"The sheep like to play chase," she said and flapped the
Frisbee she'd taken out of the bag.

The idea of his sister casting Frisbees around to entertain
one of her designer-wool sheep ought to have seemed laugh-
able. Yet it fit her entirely.

"You still have that stack over there you haven't opened."

"I think it's clothes." He hadn't missed them up until now,
which seemed like a good reason to avoid even going through
them. "Only thing I care about keeping is the wine."

Her expression softened, but he pointedly ignored it. Instead, he hastily stepped over a small mountain of crumpled
newsprint that had been wrapped around a set of dishes he
hadn't known he possessed, which Dahlia had loaded into

the dishwasher, and then he escaped out the door before she could make more of the wine situation than he wanted.

His dad gave him some of his favorite wine.

Nothing to get all worked up about.

The sun was straight up, and he blamed it for the burn in his eyes.

Squinting at the ground, he trekked around to the front of the main house to retrieve the rusty old pickup, only to stop in surprise at the sight of his mother's car just parking in the drive.

He waited while she turned off the engine and climbed out. She was dressed in black yoga pants and a snug zippered top that he supposed was meant to be a jacket. With her blond hair pulled back in a slightly messy ponytail, she could have passed for one of his sisters, versus his mother.

"What're you doing here?"

She smiled and pushed her dark glasses up onto her head. "Good morning to you, too." She stretched up and kissed his cheek. "A little birdie told me you were getting your guesthouse ready for Hope. Thought I'd come and see how it was going."

"Dahlia texted you and told you we could barely get through the door," he deciphered.

Wendy didn't deny it. "I was surprised, though. Hope's been living with you for months."

"She's been living in *my house* for months," he corrected. "Two different things."

She gave him a look. "Keep telling yourself that, honey. So, what prompted the change? Is everything okay between the two of you?"

"What do you mean *between*? We're not—"

She raised her hand. "Enough. If you want to keep your head in the sand, you're the one who gets to pick the grains out of your teeth." She tugged at the hem of her short jacket. "You know that I believe it's healthy for a woman to have a sense of independence. Just as I believe it's healthy for an individual to be honest with themselves." She shot her cuff and glanced at her diamond wristwatch. "And honesty makes me admit that I don't have time to stand here yammering. I have marketing meetings soon at the castle about the launch." She patted his cheek in obvious dismissal and strode off in the direction of the guesthouse.

He squinted into the sky. How much would his mother appreciate his honesty when he told her about the Zazlo place? He rubbed his hand down his face and yanked open the squeaking pickup truck door and coaxed the engine into starting.

Wendy was showing something on her phone to Dahlia when he pulled up at the guesthouse a few minutes later. He ignored them both in favor of loading up the truck bed and driving off with the first load. Far as he could tell, neither one of them gave him any notice.

He drove into Chatelaine and dropped the load at the thrift store, waiving off the donation receipt that one of the volunteers there wanted to give him, and made the return drive back out to the lake. The biggest nuisance was dealing with manually opening and closing the gate, which had stopped working again. Still, all told, the round trip took less than an hour, and when he got there, Dahlia and his mother had been joined by Sabrina, who was looking particularly round sitting on a stool with her arms propped over her immense belly.

At least Jade was busy with the petting zoo, he thought as he made quick work of taking off with a second load.

He loved his sisters, but when they all got together, they always fell way too easily into the "tell baby brother what to do" mode.

This time, when he returned, his sisters and mother were gone. But the furniture that had been pushed to one side of the place had been rearranged, and Hope was sitting on the short, overstuffed couch, fiddling with a bunch of orange and red wildflowers that she'd placed inside a clear mason jar. She looked across at him when he entered and pressed her fingertip to her lips.

He spotted Evie sound asleep on a blanket on the floor next to the couch, her rump stuck in the air and her little crinkly book clutched in her fist.

He ignored the hollow pang inside his chest and quietly sat down opposite them both in the side chair that was just as dated as the puffed-up couch and—he figured—just as uncomfortable.

"You'll need new furniture," he said in a low voice. "This stuff is older than I am."

"It's perfectly fine," she said, equally soft. "You just don't like the pattern of gigantic mauve and teal palm fronds."

That was true enough. "The furniture came with the place."

"Your mom mentioned that."

He lifted a brow. "You saw her, then?"

"She and Dahlia were just leaving when Evie and I got back." She fluffed the clutch of wildflowers once more and set it in the middle of the square coffee table. The flowers clashed with the overwhelming amount of teal and pink. "When you said next week, I thought you meant next weekend."

"I wanted to surprise you."

"You did." She leaned forward again to slide the mason jar to the corner of the coffee table and sat back yet again. "There're even dishes and pots and pans in the kitchen cupboard."

"And wine." The crate was still sitting where he'd left it on the breakfast bar. It seemed to be the only thing that hadn't been moved during his last trip to Chatelaine. "Did you arrange everything?"

She shook her head. "This is how the furniture was when I came in here."

Evidently, his mother's meetings at the castle hadn't been quite as imminent as she'd implied if she'd taken the time to rearrange furniture with Dahlia. It was a sure bet that Sabrina hadn't been up to moving the stuff. She'd looked like she was lucky to be able to just move herself around.

"How was the petting zoo?"

"Fine. A new potbellied pig arrived just before we left. Evie was so enthralled, it was hard to tear her away."

He glanced around the corners of the guesthouse, wondering why he'd thought this was a good idea at all.

There was no good place for Evie's crib, much less the menagerie of stuffed animals he had been giving her almost since day one.

"I didn't think of saving some of the boxes," he said. His whisper sounded more ragged than he liked. "Could have reused them to move your stuff over here."

"I don't have a lot of stuff, remember?"

As if he could forget. "More than a few laundry basketsful," he countered.

Her lips stretched slightly. "Evie has more things than I do." She moved the jar of wildflowers a third time.

Was the reality of having her own space less appealing than she'd thought?

"There's still no news about the car?"

How could he have forgotten? She, more than anyone, wanted those answers. He shook his head. "Sorry. Villanueva is still drawing a blank on it. I should have told you." The investigator had sent a text late the night before that he was done in Nebraska, having confirmed his belief that the "possibles" living there were unrelated to Hope's case. "He's gone back to Corpus already."

"I'm not any worse off with no answer now than I was before," she murmured, and brushed her hands over her jean-clad thighs as if brushing off the topic altogether. Then she stood and moved around him, coming to a stop in front of the wall adjacent to the breakfast counter. She propped her hands on her narrow hips and just stood there. Her hair was getting so long now that it reached halfway down to her waist.

He curled his fingers into a ball, trying to rid the itchy need to run them through those shining waves.

"Evie's crib could go here," she finally said, sweeping her hand in the air. "Maybe a shelf there for some of her stuffed animals and toys. Sort of like she has now?"

He got that familiar pang in his chest again.

He'd be afraid he was afflicted with some disease that caused heartburn if he didn't know that both the cause and the cure resided with her.

"Sure," he replied a little belatedly. The wall she was looking at was pale white with a distinct yellow cast. "If you want new paint, it'd be better to do it before you move in." He waited a beat, studying the ugly couch. "What about your bed?" The place didn't allow for much more furniture, and the crib would take up most of the space against the wall she was considering.

"I'll sleep on the couch for now, I guess." She walked back around him and flipped up one of the cushions to look beneath it. "Too bad it's not a hide-a-bed."

"Hide-a-beds are never comfortable."

She looked over her shoulder at him, her eyebrows lifted with skepticism. "*You* have slept in a hide-a-bed before?"

"Not specifically slept," he allowed. "But back in college there was a girl—"

"Say no more." Her cheeks pinked and she rolled her eyes. "Please."

He could feel his grin sneaking out despite his effort otherwise. "Maybe a Murphy bed would work. At least you'd have a real mattress—" He broke off when his cell phone buzzed. Pulling it from his pocket, he showed her the name on the screen.

Villanueva.

Speak of the devil.

Her eyebrows immediately pulled together, and her gaze cut to Evie still sleeping blissfully with her little book.

Ridge stood and went outside onto the porch before swiping the screen and holding the phone to his ear. "What's up?" He felt Hope come up behind him, standing close enough to feel the warmth of her.

"Finally got some useful info from one of my cop friends," Villanueva said.

He turned slightly and put his arm around Hope's shoulders, holding the phone between them so she could hear as well. "That's good." His pulse shifted into higher gear, but he kept his tone even.

"The car was rented in St. Louis at the airport," the other man continued. "Same car. Six different times over the last seven months. Driver's name was Howard Marks of Nashville, Tennessee."

Hope sank down until she was sitting on the porch step. But she shook her head slightly in response to Ridge when he immediately sat beside her. Her cool hand slid into his, and he curled his fingers around hers.

"Wife's name is Petunia." Villanueva was still speaking. "They're the only ones who match the general description your brother provided. I'm texting their DMV photos. They're nearly eight years old but I'm working on getting more recent ones."

"What's the guy's story? Who is he?"

"Don't have all of that yet," the investigator said. "Expect to by the end of the day. We're looking at the foster care angle in particular. The only thing I know so far is he's a stockbroker. But I wanted to let you know so you could run the photos by your family. I'm texting them to you now."

Right on cue, Ridge's phone pinged softly.

Hope's fingers tightened on his. Her cheeks were pale.

"Let me know if your brother recognizes them," Villanueva added.

"I will. Either way," he added, but the investigator had already ended the call.

Ridge's thumb hovered over his cell phone screen. With a simple brush, he'd be able to reveal the texted photos.

"You ready for this?" he asked Hope.

She shook her head. "But that's not a good reason to wait."

He wasn't so sure about that, but he swiped the screen and the text message opened.

The two photos were small, but remained clear enough even after he'd expanded them to fill the screen.

Howard had a head of fading brown hair and nondescript features. Petunia had darker brown hair with bangs that were cut too short over a narrow face. She was equally average looking.

He studied Hope's auburn head. "Anything?"

She took the phone from him and made the photos even larger. Swiping between Howard, then Petunia, then back again. "Nothing," she said finally and handed him back the phone. "No reaction even."

"Reaction?"

She took his free hand and pressed it to the center of her chest. "No racing heart."

Ridge couldn't say the same.

He slid his splayed fingers away from the gentle swell of her breasts and stood.

"If even my subconscious knew them, I'd have a reaction," Hope said with enviable certainty. She stood as well and swiped her hands over the seat of her jeans as she went back inside. Only then did Ridge realize that Evie was making noises.

He paced around in a circle in front of the guesthouse, squeezing the back of his neck with one hand and strangling his phone with his other hand.

Then Hope reappeared with a sleepy looking Evie in her arms. "I'm going to fix her lunch," she said and started off toward the house.

He watched her for a long moment, before forwarding the photos to Nash.

Recognize them? Old DMV photos.

Nash replied immediately.

It's them. He's nearly bald now and she had short gray hair, but I'm dead sure. Who are they?

Ridge blew out a long breath. He sent the information along to Villanueva and wished to hell he'd never offered up the guesthouse for Hope to use. She and Evie were a lot safer under his roof than they would be two hundred and fifty yards away.

He sent another text to Nash.

I'll fill you in later. But keep watch.

Then he followed behind Hope, deliberately not catching up to her before she reached the house.

She'd have been eight years younger when those photos were taken. Maybe it was the reason why she hadn't recognized either one of them. An explanation for her "no reaction."

Yet, eight years really wasn't such a long time. The annoyingly logical voice inside his head seemed determined to debate the matter.

A middle-aged person's looks didn't change *that* much in less than ten years.

How could Hope panic so much over the sight of a car, but not the images of the people who'd occupied it?

Once again, he was left with more questions than when they'd started.

And one of them now was whether or not he should tell Hope about Nash's confirmation.

Instead of going inside, he diverted around to the deck and walked all the way down to the cantilevered rail.

The lake—his portion of it, anyway—was quiet. He called Mitch's office. Not surprisingly, he wasn't available on a Monday afternoon.

Ridge left a message to call him and finally went inside.

Evie was in her high chair, shoveling her fingers through her cooked green beans in favor of the spoon that Hope was trying to use. "Come on, baby," he heard her coax, but Evie wasn't having any of it. She wanted both the spoon and to squish and squeeze her beans, and that was that.

"It'll take her two hours to eat at this rate," Hope said ruefully as she surrendered the spoon again.

"What about one of those squeeze pouches?"

"I need to pick up more from GreatStore. And it's important that she figure out the utensils, too."

He leaned down to Evie's level. "Hard being eight months old, isn't it, Little Miss?"

She grinned and tossed a handful of green beans into his face.

Hope muffled her laugh, but her eyes sparkled as she yanked a paper towel off the roll and handed it to him.

He didn't have the heart to kill that sparkle just yet. He'd wait until Villanueva found the link between Howard and Petunia Marks and Hope. Until then, he'd just have to make sure that everyone on the ranch remained vigilant.

Six times, Villanueva had said. Ridge, though, only knew of three times. Did that mean Howard and Petunia Marks had been sniffing around three other times that they hadn't known about? Or were those incidences unrelated to Hope altogether?

The likelihood of that seemed small. They'd traveled each time to St. Louis before beginning the hunt.

The location had to be significant.

Had Hope lived there? If so, how...why...had she ended up in Texas? Last month, she'd had a memory flash of riding a bus and running, somehow landing in his barn, no less, but even she had admitted the memory felt typically garbled and confusing. Like some sort of bad dream that felt real but wasn't quite.

"If you have work to do, you don't have to hang around here," Hope said. "Not on our account."

He looked at her.

"You're frowning." She waved her hand as if to encompass his entirety. "I thought it was maybe because you were thinking about everything else you have to do."

The "everything else" was already being capably taken

care of by ranch employees who'd been there well before his family had come along.

But now that Hope had pointed out his frown, he realized that his jaw was so tight it ached, and no amount of willpower let it ease up. But it was easier letting her believe he was thinking about work than worrying about her. "How about a trip to the hardware store?" he suggested abruptly.

Her eyebrows lifted.

"You can choose paint colors for the guesthouse." And he could get the parts to fix the gate opener for once and for all.

She angled her head, and her hair slid over her shoulder. "I suppose you think it'll be necessary to hire a painter again like you did with the nursery."

It was exactly what he'd been thinking. "That *is* how the paint gets on the walls."

"You are such a Richie Rich." Her smile widened. "You're a *Ridgy Rich*." She actually giggled. "We could paint it ourselves you know. It's not that much work. And I already know what colors I want for Evie's wall. The same colors she has now."

"Hiring professional painters helps keep the economy turning," he defended.

She laughed outright, and Evie joined in, adding the accompaniment of drumming her spoon against her high chair tray.

The ache in his jaw suddenly eased.

Amazing what a little laughter from his ladies could do.

Chapter Twelve

They spent the rest of the day painting the guesthouse walls.

To be strictly accurate, Hope spent the day painting while Ridge—after banishment from ever touching a paintbrush or roller again—spent it keeping Evie occupied.

"You should have said the real reason you wanted to hire painters was because you'd never done it before," Hope told him when she finally climbed down from the ladder after repainting over his apparently subpar attempts.

"I've painted before," he defended.

She pressed her lips together. "Okay," she said after a moment. "It's just not everyone's forte."

He might have felt more crestfallen if he'd cared a jot about his skill as a housepainter. "You're not perfect, either."

Her lips parted, and she whirled around to face the wall that was an almost exact replica of the nursery in the house. There was no wainscoting, but she'd done some magic with painter's tape and the two colors of paint—blush above and rosemary below—looked just as good. "Did I really miss a spot?" She started up the ladder again. "I'm certain I didn't get any paint on the ceiling like you did."

He chuckled and caught her around the waist, lifting her off the ladder. "The walls are perfect," he assured. "It's *you* who's got the spots." He slowly let her slide through his arms until her feet touched the ground. Then he lifted her chin and took the damp rag out of her fist to wipe her chin.

"Oh, well. Getting paint on myself is okay," she said, though she sounded decidedly breathless.

He rubbed another spatter from her temple. "You have some in your hair, too," he murmured, *finally* threading his fingers through her hair that she'd smoothed back into a long ponytail.

Her lashes fluttered closed, and her hands clasped his shoulders. "It'll wash out in the shower," she breathed.

He was an idiot, was what he was. Lighting matches even though he knew better than to start this particular fire. "You might need help."

Brilliant blue peeked at him from beneath her long lashes, and she leaned into him. Her lips parted softly, and she rocked her hips ever so slightly against him. "I might," she agreed.

He almost groaned aloud and clamped his hands on her hips to stop the maddening motion. At least that was his intention. But good intentions were futile when she was stretching up against him, her hands sliding from his shoulders to his neck, and her fingers roved through his hair as if they'd felt just as greedy for the sensation as he had. Her breasts were flattened against him. He could feel the point of her tight nipples and the unevenness of her breath.

Evie was fed and safely confined in her play yard with her stack of toys, and all it would take would be a second to rid himself and Hope of a few pieces of clothing to feel every inch of her against him.

He kissed her temple. His fingers drifted to the hem of her T-shirt. Slid beneath. Her skin was like velvet. Warm. Smooth. Enticing.

She made a soft *mmm* sound that went straight to his head,

and he dragged aside the stretchy fabric cup of her bra to palm her breast. She moaned a little more, and he lowered his mouth to take that tight nipple between his lips, T-shirt and all.

Her moan turned to a throaty groan, and when she dragged his free hand to her other breast, he was nearly undone.

"Don't stop," she begged.

He wasn't sure he could even if he wanted.

And he seriously didn't want to.

He yanked her shirt upward, and she accommodated by lifting her arms. As soon as the fabric cleared her head, he sent it sailing while he lowered his head to her neck. The warm curve of her shoulder. Down to the valley between her breasts, still plumped up from the bra cups he'd pulled aside. Her skin was creamy...her nipples rosy and rigid. He circled one with his thumb while he tasted the other, and she cried out.

He paused instantly, not sure he hadn't hurt her.

"Don't stop," she gasped again. Her lips were parted. Her cheeks flushed. He dragged his thumbs slowly over her nipples again, and the flush deepened.

She writhed against him.

He'd never seen anything more arousing.

Ridge turned and lifted her to the back of the ugly sofa that they'd pushed away from the wall and to the center of the room, and she dragged at his shirt. He yanked it off and sent it the way of hers. She immediately pressed her mouth against his chest and linked her ankles behind him, tightening him into the V of her thighs. He ran his hands down her back. Up her sides. Felt her shiver. But he knew now that her nipples were the fuse to fireworks.

He was more than ready to set that flame...but in time.

For now, he drew the cups of her bra down a little more

and her breathing quickened. He tasted the creamy flesh. Kissed his way from one mound to the other, and her inhalation was a hiss when his lips barely whispered over the tight peaks.

Her head fell back, and she rocked against him.

"You're going to come, aren't you," he whispered against the pulse throbbing madly in her throat. "If I do this." Light as air, he drifted his fingers over her nipples.

She groaned. "Ridge, please."

It was the only kind of begging he ever wanted to hear come from her lips. "I don't have to touch you anywhere else," he rasped. "Just—" he drifted again, barely a whisper of a touch "—there."

Her mouth was open. Her body quivered. "Don't tease."

"Not a tease," he assured. "A promise."

Blue fire looked up at him through her lashes. "Prove it," she said throatily.

The need inside him was feral. He lowered his mouth to her breast, watching her all the while. He didn't touch her, though. Just breathed on that sweet, tight, ruby peak.

"You're going to pay for this," she promised huskily.

He smiled slowly. "Now who's the tease?"

"Oh, it's a promise," she said.

He touched the tip of his tongue to her nipple.

She jerked, and he felt the ripple that worked through her abdomen.

"More?"

She nodded restlessly. "A lot more."

He laughed soundlessly and circled all the way around. Drew it lightly between his lips while his fingertip flirted with the other.

Hope's breathing was almost a sob. Her legs were a vise around his hips.

"More?" he asked again.

She didn't answer. Just lifted her hand to his and boldly pressed his thumb and index finger around her nipple.

Fire licked down his spine. If he wasn't careful, he would beat her to the fireworks.

He caught her nipple between his teeth and bathed her with his tongue while he gently compressed the other, until he finally cupped both her breasts, squeezing her nipples tightly between his fingers, and he found her mouth with his.

She convulsed, her pleasure seeming to go on and on before she collapsed bonelessly in his arms.

His own breath was raging from his chest, and he lifted her onto the couch, nearly falling over her. Their hands collided as they worked at their jeans, and then she was guiding him into her and they both groaned. Everything about her was exactly perfect for him. She wound around him, her mouth on his. "Faster," she begged.

What else could he do but comply? Particularly when her hands were racing over him, threading through his hair, and she was murmuring his name as though it was the only name in the world for her.

And then she was quaking around him all over again, and if he'd ever had any fantasies about making this last, they went right out the window as he succumbed to the mindless perfection of his Hope.

He was still panting like he'd climbed Everest when she shoved at his shoulders a short time later. "Did you hear that?"

All he could hear was his heart still clanging inside his head. He kissed the tiny birthmark on her neck. "No."

"Anyone home?"

He jerked his head up, too.

Met Hope's wide blue gaze.

Her cheeks were red from razor burn. Her lips almost swollen from his kisses. He pressed her head down to the cushion and out of sight and looked almost fatalistically at the door. Just waiting for the knob to turn.

Which it did.

Then the door opened, and Jade stood there in the wash of the porch light. "I knew you had to be somewhere around here," she said, as if there was nothing at all unusual over finding her brother sitting on an ugly mauve and teal couch partially shrouded in plastic drop cloths without a shirt.

Their only saving grace was the fact that the couch was facing away from the front door.

Jade had no way of seeing that he didn't have anything else on, either, and that Hope was still mostly underneath him.

"Oh," his sister said, as if she'd just realized something.

Ridge's neck burned, but then he noticed her attention on Evie's play yard near the door and the fact that she'd fallen asleep amongst her toys.

Jade pressed her finger to her lips. "Sorry," she whispered. "I'll wait over at the house." She slowly pulled the door closed again, and the breath that he hadn't realized he was holding escaped.

He sat back against one arm of the couch and raked his hand through his hair while Hope untangled her legs from his. She set her bra to rights and slid down to her hands and knees on the floor to crawl after her clothes.

"I don't think Jade's going to look through the windows," he said.

Hope just gave him a harried grimace before she yanked her T-shirt on and tugged her ponytail free of the neckline. Flinging his shirt in his direction, she slid on her jeans and then pulled up her knees, wrapping her arms around her legs. She lowered her head. "This is mortifying." Her voice was muffled.

"Why?"

She lifted her head just long enough to give him a scandalized glare before dropping her forehead back to her knees again.

He stiffly got to his feet and yanked his jeans back on. Shaking out his shirt, he saw the splotches of dried paint on the front.

He figured not even Terralee's talents would be enough to save the thing. "At least Evie fell asleep," he said as he pulled the shirt over his head.

Hope groaned, and this time there was nothing erotic about it at all.

He went to the door. "I'll go deal with my sister."

"Good luck."

The house was only a few minutes away. He wished it was farther.

He went in through the back kitchen door. Jade was sitting at the island.

"This is becoming a habit." He closed the door behind him.

"Yeah, and I had to drive around the back sides of our property to get here. Did you know your gate opener isn't working?"

"I'll get it fixed," he told her.

"Soon, I hope," she groused, pushing a shoebox-sized plastic container toward him.

He reached instead for the refrigerator door and pulled out a beer. "What's that?" He gestured with the bottom of the bottle toward the box before taking a quick drink, then following it with a near guzzle.

Jade noticed and raised her eyebrows. "Hard day?"

"Implying that my work isn't taxing enough these days to qualify as hard?"

"Good grief." Her eyebrows went even higher. "I wasn't even remotely thinking that." She shook her head slightly. "When did you get so touchy?"

"I'm not touchy," he denied and lifted the bottle again. "What's in the box?"

"Family photos." Jade was still giving him a strange look, but apparently her agenda was already full enough without adding the task of figuring out what was stuck under Ridge's saddle. "Therefore—" she jabbed a finger in the air between them "—I don't want to hear any more excuses about not having a photo to give as a wedding present to our mystery couple."

That stupid wedding had been about the furthest thing from Ridge's mind.

His sister dropped her finger to the box and pushed it toward him. "Pick one. Any one. I don't care which." She looked beyond him, and he realized that Hope—mortification be damned—had followed him through the back door. She was carrying a still-sleeping Evie and walked past them both, disappearing down the hall.

She returned a few minutes later. "A successful transfer to the crib," she said. "Amazingly enough." Her eyes bounced between Jade and Ridge before she turned away and yanked open the refrigerator door with only a small clatter of bottles inside. "Can I get you something to drink, Jade?"

"I'm fine."

Hope extracted a bottle of water and pushed the door closed with her hip. She maintained a healthy distance between herself and Ridge as she moved to the other side of the island. Aside from a few wrinkles on her T-shirt, there was no evidence that, not too long ago, Ridge had kissed his way through the cloth long enough to leave a wet mark on it.

"I just brought these by for Ridge." Jade tapped the plastic container. "Will you make sure he chooses a photo before the mystery wedding?" She didn't wait for an answer and looked back at Ridge. "You can return the box to me later."

"Fine. Whatever," he said.

"Happy day. Aren't you all agreeable now?" She took the beer bottle from him only long enough to look at the label. "Fortune's Rising IPA." Her lips twitched. "Figures." She handed it back to him. "I'm introducing the new potbellied pig in the morning at the petting zoo. We're definitely going with your idea of holding a contest to name him. Will you be coming by?"

Ridge didn't make the mistake of thinking she was addressing him. Hope was the one who took Evie down to his sister's passion project every day.

She was nodding as she pulled an apron over her head and tied the strings around her waist. "We should be there right after opening time. If I have some ideas for names, can I participate, or am I disqualified because I know you?"

Jade laughed as she headed for the door. "Hardly. I just want a fun event that garners interest in the petting zoo. The more proceeds we make, the more kids we can accommodate in our free workshops," she said on her way out.

Ridge pulled out a bar stool and sat. The ever-present mason jar sat on the island, filled with several gray-green stalks. He absently pulled the jar closer and sniffed the tight buds.

Lavender.

He didn't even know where lavender was growing around here any more than he knew where the orange and red flowers she'd placed in the guesthouse came from, but he knew

Hope was forever finding one sort or another. He moved the jar aside and reached for the photos, flipping off the lid. With little interest, he pulled out a stack of color snapshots and started flipping through them. "Potbellied pig names, huh?"

"You bet." Hope sounded determinedly breezy. She set an oversize bowl on the counter and opened another cupboard, pulling out a hand mixer. "Torvis." She opened a drawer. Dropped the metal beaters she extracted on the butcher-block top. "George the Great. Donald."

Ridge smiled. "Do you always have a stockpile of names at your fingertips?"

She opened the pantry and hefted out an enormous canister. "Just for pigs, I think." She set the canister next to the bowl and rummaged in another drawer until she came up with a metal measuring cup. "Choosing Evie's name was a much lengthier pro—"

The measuring cup clattered to the floor.

Her eyes were saucers when they turned his way. "Rebecca," she whispered. "Amelia. Danny wanted—" Her face paled even more, and she swayed a little. "Petal." The word came out through clenched teeth as she pressed her hands to both sides of her head as if pained.

He dropped the handful of photographs and caught her just in time to save her from crumbling when her knees went out from beneath her. Sweeping her up in his arms, he carried her to the couch, kneeling down to deposit her.

Her eyes were closed.

His phone.

Where the hell was his phone?

He swore and pressed his knuckles lightly against her pallid cheek. It was cool. Vaguely clammy.

Or maybe that was just him.

He'd forgotten all about the landline. That's how dependent he was on his cell phone. But there was the cordless phone sitting in its cradle practically in front of his nose on a side table. He snatched it up and returned to the couch, kneeling on the floor next to her while he made sure there was a dial tone before he started to punch out 911 with his thumb.

With his other hand, he yanked at the strings of the chef's apron she had tied around her waist in accordance with some deeply buried factoid to remove constrictions when a person fainted.

Hope's hand drifted over his arm. "Stop," she whispered.

Her eyes were slits of bruised periwinkle looking up at him.

He didn't punch out the last number, but he held on to the phone, anyway. His fingers were clamped around the hard, oddly substantial handset so tightly they wouldn't have obeyed any sort of command to loosen.

"I'm okay," she continued, still in a whisper that seemed like she was anything *but* okay. "Danny wanted to name the baby Petal, after his mother. It was better than Petunia."

Puzzle pieces fell into place.

If his head wasn't pounding with his own pulse, he would have probably heard the sound of them all clicking together. Completing the picture of Hope's real story.

Real family.

"Danny's mother." He managed to get the words out through a throat that felt as locked up as his fingers.

"Danny Marks." Her face crumpled, and she began crying softly. "My husband."

Chapter Thirteen

Hope felt Ridge's arms come around her and even though she knew she ought to be stronger, she clung to him as the tears racked through her. Tears for the past. For the present. For the future that would never be.

She cried until there was nothing left inside her but a hiccup and a stitch in her side and the front of Ridge's shirt was damp and wrinkled.

His gaze was dark and searching when she finally made herself push away from him. She only got as far as the corner of the couch, though. She didn't seem to have the strength to go any further.

She didn't know if she appreciated the fact that he didn't say a word or if it would have been easier if he'd started peppering her with questions.

That's what Danny would have done.

She closed her eyes again and rubbed her cheeks. "I'm sorry," she said thickly.

"Don't be sorry."

"I remember everything."

Ridge's expression didn't change, but he seemed to tense. Or maybe that was just her.

She ducked her head, using the hem of her shirt to wipe at her cheeks even though his shirt had already absorbed the brunt of her tears.

He got up and went to the kitchen, returning a moment later with a damp towel. He rolled it into a compress then tucked his hand beneath her chin and gently swiped her face with it.

She nearly started crying all over again and to stop it, simply pressed the whole damp bundle against her eyes. "My head is pounding." It wasn't untrue, but it was still just an excuse to put off the inevitable.

"I'm calling Mitch."

She lifted the compress to look at him. "I don't need a doctor."

But he'd already reached for the phone again and began dialing. "Mitch or 911. Humor me."

She chewed the inside of her cheek and applied the damp compress to her closed eyes again while he spoke briefly into the phone.

"He's on his way," he said.

Then silence stretched between them and it felt like a living thing, pulsing right along with the rhythmic pounding inside her head.

She lifted the compress once more and waved it in the air. "Who knew the key to my memory would be a pig-naming contest?" Her desperate attempt at flippancy fell miserably flat.

The corners of Ridge's mouth lifted slightly, but not even he could keep up the pretense. "Want to tell me about... Danny?"

Was it her imagination that he'd hesitated before speaking her husband's name?

Hearing him say it made her wince slightly.

And no, she didn't want to tell him about Danny. She didn't even want to think about Danny. But of course, that seemed almost all she could do.

Every single detail had come pouring back. Just as Mitch had suggested it would. The whole lot swung from one side of her mind to another with the delicacy of a wrecking ball.

The good.

The bad.

The tragic.

She unfolded the towel. Refolded it. Then just twisted it together between her hands. "My name is Holly," she said instead.

Holly.

Marks.

Her name joined the pounding inside her head.

"My mother was fifteen when she had me and sixteen when she dumped me off at a fire station." She grimaced. "Not that I remember it."

Ridge's features tightened. "You were an infant. But you ended up in group homes?"

There were more important things to tell him. Life-changing things to tell him. "I guess I was sort of sickly. That's the reason I was never adopted. At least that's the story I got." She realized she was picking at her thumb, creating a hangnail where there'd been none and made herself stop. "I was with a bunch of different foster families. Nobody lasted more than a few years."

He muttered something under his breath. Shook his head. "I'm sorry," he said.

"For all I know, it might have been worse if she'd tried to keep me," she said. She'd never really hated her mother for abandoning her when she'd been just a child, herself. Holly had learned quickly enough that her situation was better than some.

But that didn't mean she hadn't longed for a family of her own.

A real family.

The image of Danny's face swam inside her head and her stomach churned.

She pressed the compress against her face again, swallowing down the wave of nausea.

Then the doorbell chimed and Ridge bolted off the couch again. "Finally."

He sounded as anxious to escape as she felt.

Yet, after escorting Mitch inside, he didn't leave them alone. Choosing instead to pace around the couch while his friend sat down beside her and gave her a calm smile. "How're you doing?"

She gave him a shrug. She was busy watching Ridge from the corner of her eyes.

What was he thinking?

She realized Mitch had opened his medical bag and was pulling out his stethoscope and blood pressure cuff. She chewed the inside of her cheek, enduring his attention and counting her way through the blood pressure check, as if she could control the results with a slow, measured one-to-ten. He pulled out a light and shined it in her eyes, asked her if she had any pain—she did, but not the kind that he could help with—and then returned everything to his bag again and just sat there for a moment, watching her.

"Are you okay staying here now?"

The question surprised her as much as it did Ridge.

"Why the hell wouldn't she be," he demanded.

Mitch just raised his eyebrows slightly at his friend, who seemed to take whatever message that was meant to convey, and started pacing again, with a fresh rhythmic flexing of his jaw.

"I'm fine," she answered belatedly, realizing that Mitch was still waiting for her answer. Aside from a massive headache, the emotional pain that surpassed it wasn't something that a pill was going to help.

Another wave of tears was building behind her eyes and she pinched her eyes shut. She couldn't do a thing to stop the hitch in her breath, though.

She'd tried so hard to make everything better, to disastrous effect.

"I can give you a sedative—"

She shook her head hard. So many times she'd heard that offer back then. After the accident. Didn't matter that she'd been pregnant—

A piercing cry erupted from the baby monitor, seeming to make them all jump.

She snatched up the monitor and muted the volume.

Ridge took a step away from the fireplace. "I'll get—"

"No!" She shoved the monitor into his hands, pretending not to see the frown on his face. "She needs feeding." She practically ran from the room, but not fast enough to miss the cautioning grip that Mitch took on Ridge's arm when he would have followed her.

Tears leaked down her face as she closed herself in the nursery with Evie, who wailed even louder and stretched out her arms.

"I know, baby." She lifted her daughter out of the crib and pressed her face to her sweet cheek, hauling in a shuddering breath. "Everything's going to be okay."

Considering the tumult of memories accosting her, the assurance was hollow, but Evie didn't know that.

Or maybe she did, because it took her daughter longer than usual to settle down back to sleep after feeding and it took three tries before she settled back down to sleep after an exhausted sigh.

Hope wished she could remain in the nursery forever, but

of course, she couldn't. She went into the en suite bathroom and snatched a tissue from the box. She blew her nose for what felt like the hundredth time. She splashed cool water over her face in hopes of alleviating the red circles around her eyes.

But when she straightened and looked in the mirror, she still looked a wreck.

As if there'd been no passage of time at all since that last, dreadful argument with Danny.

Fourteen months ago.

How much had occurred in that span of time?

It was no time at all, and yet an entire lifetime.

Evie's, at any rate.

She slid open a drawer and stared hollowly at the contents.

Hairbrush. Ponytail holders. Tweezers and face cream and a small quilted cosmetic case that Wendy Fortune herself had given Hope.

"Just a few things," she'd said only a few days after they'd met and she'd come to visit Ridge, bearing a bag of things for the baby and the little quilted case for Hope. "Essentials that every girl needs." Wendy's smile had been almost unbearably kind. Lip gloss. A tube of mascara. Blush. And a wad of twenty-dollar bills that Hope hadn't touched until Christmas arrived and she'd still had no memory of who she was, and a stronger desire to purchase a few gifts than to keep from touching that money because of pride.

She pulled out the brush and drew it almost manically through her hair until her scalp tingled and the strands were crackling with static electricity. Then she raked it all back again in a tight ponytail.

But it only accentuated the pinched lines around her eyes and mouth, and she let it down again.

She knew she was wasting time, hiding in the bathroom.

Knew that Ridge was out there, waiting. Questions still dammed up in his beautiful brown eyes.

She opened the cosmetic case from Wendy. The distinctive blue box inside contained the diamond key necklace that Ridge had given her, tucked in the very same spot that had once held the wad of twenties.

With trembling fingers, she thumbed open the jewelry box and traced the outline of the key with the tip of her fingernail. The diamonds winked softly.

She closed the box. Pulled out the blush and smoothed some on her pale cheeks. It wasn't much in the way of armor, but it helped just a little.

Selfishly she wished that her daughter would start fussing again. Offer up a reasonable reason for Hope to stay in the nursery.

Not Hope.

Holly.

Another numbingly loud metronome took up residence inside her head, and she pressed her fingers against her aching temples.

Only a few hours ago, Ridge had given her the most intense orgasms she'd ever had in her life.

She was every bit the horrible person that Petunia and Howard believed her to be.

Just go out there, Hope. Tell Ridge the truth.

That you're the reason your husband is dead.

She let out a deep, shuddering breath.

Avoiding her reflection in the mirror, she returned everything inside the quilted case, zipped it shut and closed the drawer. Then she turned off the light and left the bathroom.

Mitch was gone. No surprise. And Ridge was sitting on the couch but there was nothing relaxed in his demeanor. As soon as he heard her, he rose. His gaze searching.

So close, she thought with a deepening ache inside. She'd been so close to real happiness with him. And now—

"Evie okay?"

She nodded.

His jaw shifted. "And you?"

This time, her nod was jerky. She sat on the arm of a side chair and tucked her hands beneath her thighs to hide the way they'd started trembling again.

Just tell him.

"I thought I could take Evie to Mexico," she blurted baldly. "I had my passport and a little cash with me." What she'd managed to hide away without Danny's knowledge before she'd even become pregnant. "I took a half dozen different buses from St. Louis to hide our trail. By the time I reached Texas, I thought we were nearly home free." She pressed her lips together against an ugly wave of nausea. "Obviously I was wrong."

"Why were you heading to Mexico?"

"Because Howard and Petunia were going to take Evie from me."

She realized she was too restless to sit.

Instead, she stood and paced across the room, tucking her shaking hands in her back pockets. She stared blindly at the artful arrangement of books and candles on one end of the mantel. Terralee's doing.

Hope's—*Holly's*—contribution to the household had mostly been limited to jars of wildflowers that she stole from the roadside.

"Why do you think they were going to take Evie from you?"

"I *know* they were going to," she corrected. "I had pounds of paperwork from the attorneys who told me so."

"But why?"

"Because I'm not a suitable mother."

"Bullshit."

She winced a little. Not so much at the word but at the passion in the delivery.

Her eyes burned. She was still facing the mantel. Easier that way. She couldn't look at him and tell him the truth. To see the warmth in his expression wither and die.

Get it over with.

Rip off the bandage and be done with it.

"They knew I caused Danny's death," she said thinly.

"He's dead then. You weren't mistaken after all." Ridge moved around to stand in front of the fireplace where she couldn't avoid seeing him. "You're *not* married." His tone was neutral, but she could see the effort it cost in the white line of his rigid jaw. "You're a widow?"

She nodded, pinching her eyes closed. Ridge's image was seared in her mind anyway. "A car accident."

"An accident is an accident. How'd you cause it?"

"A car wreck," she said. "I should have been more specific."

"It still doesn't mean it was your fault."

She opened her eyes again, throwing out an arm. "Tell your investigator my real name. That I used to live in St. Louis. Tell him about Howard and Petunia. He'll confirm it all."

"He already knows about Howard and Petunia Marks. At least he knows they were the ones driving the rental car."

Right. The investigator had told them about the car earlier that day. He'd sent the old DMV photos of Danny's parents. She ought to have recognized them, even though they'd both aged a lot by the time she'd met them.

Villanueva's text message seemed so long ago, though.

Before the hardware store.

Before the painting.

Before.

She wrapped her arms around her waist, trying to staunch the ache she felt inside. She was trembling so badly her teeth were chattering. "We were at one of Danny's endless work parties. He'd been drinking. I hadn't."

"Because you were pregnant."

She nodded. "It was t-time to leave, and I wanted to drive, but to Danny that was tantamount to saying he couldn't. Not just a basic fact that he *shouldn't*. He'd already been complaining all night about the amount of starch I'd let the dry cleaners use on his dress shirt." Recounting the utter ridiculousness of it stirred up the resentment and powerlessness she'd felt then. "As if a random wrinkle was the reason one of his c-clients hadn't shown up to the party. And I lost it." She shuddered, and Ridge flipped a switch near the mantel almost roughly.

A small flame immediately licked its way around the gas logs in the fireplace.

She moved jerkily closer to the heat. "I s-stood there on the sidewalk outside the f-fanciest hotel in the c-city and screamed at him like a lunatic until a security guard had to separate us.

"Like all things Danny, though—" she lifted her shaking hands slightly "—he talked his way out of it. The s-security guard gave Danny his keys and then he put me in a taxi. I got home. Danny didn't. He ran off an overpass."

"I'm sorry." Ridge turned up the gas flame even more. It burned hotter. Brighter. Then he braced his hand on the mantel. "That must have been awful."

Her nose felt like fire ants were crawling inside it. She focused on Ridge's hand. The long fingers. Square palm. The ridge of calluses that belied the fancy gold watch on his perfectly shaped wrist.

"I was relieved," she whispered. *That* was what was awful.

Ridge's fingers curled until his knuckles whitened. "Then he *was* mistreating you."

Her knees felt like jelly. The warmth from the fireplace had been immediate, but it didn't help her vibrating bones.

She angled sideways and slid down onto one of the armchairs that flanked the hearth. "Danny was a stockbroker. Like his father. Only we lived in St. Louis because Danny didn't like Tennessee. It was far enough away—"

She cleared the growing knot from her throat. Far enough away to keep his parents from getting too close a look at their son. She realized it now. But hindsight was always clearer, wasn't it?

"He said he wanted to move far enough away to be outside the range of his father's influence," she managed evenly. "So that he could be sure his success would be *his*."

"Was he? Successful?"

She chewed the inside of her lip. "From the outside, I'm sure we looked like the perfect couple. Handsome stockbroker and the little wife. Living in their brand-new, perfectly lovely house. Large enough to be impressive, but not so large that it was ostentatious." She looked down at her hand. Remembering the enormous diamond ring that had turned out to be fake when she'd tried to pawn it.

As if he'd known she would try to do so at some point.

"Having a lovely house doesn't guarantee everything going on inside of it is lovely, too." Ridge blew out a rough breath. "My family is proof of that."

"Did your family control every minute of your day? Twenty-four seven?"

"I think you already know they didn't." He was silent for a moment. "How long ago was the accident?"

She leaned her elbows on her knees and pressed her face to her hands. "Fourteen months."

"You must have barely been pregnant."

"I wasn't even three months along." Danny had been crowing about her pregnancy to everyone they knew from the moment the test stick had turned positive. A month later at his funeral, they'd all been whispering how tragic it all was.

It *had* been tragic.

And avoidable if she'd have just faced the truth and escaped before it had been too late.

She'd been the proverbial frog in the kettle—not smart enough to recognize the water surrounding her was getting hotter by the day.

She thrust her fingertips through her hair, digging her fingertips into her scalp. "I was stupid enough to think being pregnant might change things. But I should have known better. I'd already quit my job at the day care center because he didn't want me to work. Not even the fact that they wanted me to take over for the director who was retiring made any difference to him." She deepened her voice. "Any wife of Danny Marks will never need to work."

She yanked on her hair as she raked it back from her face. Pulling tightly because the pain of it was more welcome than the memories. "When you're young, it might sound romantic. But in reality?" She sniffed. "The one thing in my life that I'd accomplished on my own, and I gave it up without so much as a whimper. People like Danny don't change," she said huskily. "They just get more so." And she'd been no better. Just taking the blows that life kept giving her.

"You didn't answer if he was successful."

She grimaced and looked at Ridge. Her eyes felt gritty, but she could still see that he'd already come to his own—correct—conclusion.

"Everything was appearances for Danny. Including his career." She moistened her lips. "The house was mortgaged beyond its worth. The fancy car was a lease. He was a stock-broker, alright, but not a very good one. His parents never saw that, though. He was their only child. They believed he hung the moon and the stars."

"How did the two of you meet?"

"A coffee shop of all places." She shook her head. "I had just turned twenty-two. He was thirty. It was like something out of a romantic movie, and I fell, hook, line and sinker. We were married in less than six months." She made a face. "I'd say let that be a cautionary tale to all young women, except I'm the perfect example of how pointless caution-ary tales are."

She leaned forward and dropped her voice to a facetious whisper. "The big secret is that we ignore them. Every. Sin-gle. Time."

He didn't smile. Proof that he couldn't relate to a twenty-two-year-old girl who watched too many romantic comedies. "Back to the parents," he prompted instead.

"They swooped in after the funeral. At first it was a re-lief. They took care of everything. Arranged the funeral. I didn't know how to do any of that. And then they insisted that I go back to Nashville with them. Saying I was family. Carrying their only grandchild. They wanted to take care of me, too. So. I went."

She pinched back the tears collecting in her eyes. "I never had a family. Then there was Danny. And after him, there were his parents. But I hadn't learned my lesson enough. I had to wait until Evie was born to realize how insidious their helpfulness really was. And then they talked about how much more they could do for Evie than I could, especially knowing how my background hadn't taught me anything about being a proper mother, and suddenly there were legal papers getting drawn up. And Petunia reminding me that if I'd have been a better wife, Danny wouldn't have died, and—"

"Enough." Ridge crouched in front of her. "Look at me."

She shook her head.

But he gently clasped her face between his palms. Those large square palms with calluses that ought to have felt rough but didn't. "Look at me, Hope."

"Holly," she said thickly, but she focused on his face. Felt herself start to slide down into his warm brown eyes.

He brushed his thumb against her cheek, wiping away a tear. "You'll always be Hope to me. I'm in love with you, you know."

She drew in a jagged, stuttering breath. "No. I c-can't do this now."

"I'm not asking you to do anything," he said. "I'm just telling you the truth."

She couldn't form a single, coherent thought.

And maybe he realized it. Because he just lifted her hands and kissed her knuckles lightly before dragging the chair on the other side of the hearth closer.

He sat on the edge of the cushion, not even ten inches away from her. She could feel the warmth of him. But he didn't touch her.

For once, she was grateful for that.

"Tell me how you ended up in my barn."

It was a logical question.

But still she hadn't expected it. A few weeks ago, she'd already had a flashback about buses and panic and running. "You already know—"

"Go through it again," he said. "Step by step. Break it down."

"Break down more stupidity on my part?"

"Hope," he chided softly.

Holly.

She didn't voice the correction.

"The bus I was on made a stop near the LC Club. A bunch of us who'd been on the ride the longest got off to stretch our legs. We'd done it dozens of times before. I had Evie in the carrier. It was hotter than blazes. We all left our backpacks behind on the bus. The driver would lock the door. And that's what I did. Left my backpack. Which had my passport. My money."

"Someone stole it?"

"That would be pathetic, right?"

He sighed. "I once had my wallet stolen out of a gym locker I forgot to lock. It happens."

She wasn't sure she believed him. But she didn't mind so much if he was making it up to make her feel better.

Proof that she was still a sucker for self-delusion.

"I'm twenty-six, by the way," she said abruptly. "Old enough to know better."

He slid a lock of her hair away from her cheek and tucked it behind her ear. Then his hand fell away again. He waited.

Quiet.

Patient.

The Ridge who didn't seem rigid at all.

"Anyway, it wasn't stolen," she said. "Not in the true sense of the word. But while we were stretching our legs, I saw Howard and Petunia. They were in a gray rental car, pulling up almost right next to the bus. And I panicked. You know that ice cream place on the shoreline walk? Just down a ways from the LC Club."

He nodded.

"I ducked in there with Evie. I could see them from the window. They finally pulled into the parking lot at the LC

Club, but by then my bus—along with every measly dollar I possessed—left without me."

He made a soft groan. "Seriously."

"I know. It's one disaster after another."

"Those disasters brought you and Evie into my life," he said gruffly. "You'll have to pardon me for having a different take on it."

Despite everything, something dangerously sweet squiggled around inside her chest, and it alarmed the daylights out of her.

It was all she could do not to snatch Evie from her crib and bolt all over again.

"So." Ridge's steady, calm voice lured her thoughts back down from the panic level. "You saw Howard and Petunia. And their rental car. Always gray. Sounds a little OCD to me. What's the deal with that?"

"It's not OCD. It's the contract Howard's company has with the rental car company. All they have are gray sedans. Part of the *brand*." She put air quotes around the word.

"Keep it simple, stupid," Ridge murmured. "It wouldn't have mattered what the license plates on the car was, so long as it was the right color."

"I knew I needed to catch up to the bus. I realize now that the nightmares I have sometimes of running are running after that big, lumbering bus." She blew out a sigh. "Someone in the ice cream shop said the bus route always took it to Chatelaine Hills for a stop before it headed to San Antonio. I bummed a ride with some kid who looked barely legal to drive, and he let me off near the stop. It's right at the turnoff to your family's ranch."

"There's a bus stop there?"

"Quite a popular one." Some vestiges of humor twisted dryly inside of her. "For those of the non-Ridgy-Rich variety."

"Just finish the story."

"It had been a longshot in the first place. I missed the bus by nearly a half hour. By then it was starting to get late. Evie was fussing. I walked until I found a private enough spot to stop and nurse her. And then—" she shook her head again "—that bloody gray car came trolling down the road. I knew it wasn't safe to stay near the road like I had been, so I started cutting across the fields."

She tried to remember her path all those months ago and thought she must have somehow skirted to the farthest boundary of Jade's property, then angled across the somewhat wedged-shaped back sides of Nash's and Arlo's places, before finding a shelter that hadn't been lit by fancy security lights.

The clearest memory of all was the panic that had been driving her.

"When it was too dark to go any further, I ducked into what I *thought* was an empty barn. And then I heard some voices and—" she spread her palms "—the next thing I remember, I was waking up with you and Dahlia hovering over me, and everything else was just…gone."

A muscle ticked in his jaw. "You know how lucky you were to end up somewhere safe?"

"Yes. If Howard and Petunia had found me, I'd have been the living proof of their claim that I wasn't fit to raise my own child. I had no money. No roof, no food—" She broke off when he took her hands in his and squeezed slightly.

"That's not the case anymore," he reminded her. "Not only do you have food and shelter, but you've got a support system. People—not just me—who care about you. Our lawyers can—"

"No."

He gave her a look. "They're the ones who brought lawyers

into it, sweetheart. The best way to deal with them is with better lawyers. And we've got plenty of them."

Her nerves felt suddenly pinched. "I don't need you fighting my battles, Ridge!"

"Well, *somebody* better," he countered, sounding suddenly a lot less calm and reasonable. "Villanueva found them already. It's only a matter of time before the reverse is true and Howie and Pet talk to the right person who remembers seeing you or Evie. And then what are you going to do? Mexico's out, babe. No passport."

She yanked her hands from his and shoved to her feet. "Don't call me babe. My name is Hope! Ach! Holly." She waved him off. "And don't touch me right now, either. You're the reason why I can't think straight."

He lifted his hands away from her.

Once again, Evie started wailing. She hadn't remained settled after all, and the sound was magnified several times over by the assortment of baby monitors lying around.

She spun on her heel and started to head down the hallway.

"This will seem easier tomorrow." His deep, husky voice followed her.

"Easy for you to say. You don't have a child of your own that someone's threatening to take." She pushed open Evie's nursery door and went inside.

She never heard Ridge's response.

"Sure feels like I do."

Chapter Fourteen

"Morning." Beau Weatherly lifted his mug of coffee in greeting when Ridge slumped down at his table in the Daily Grind.

Ridge buried his nose in his own coffee and grunted.

"Is it Zane Baston putting in an offer on Nonny's place yesterday that's got you so chipper or the new living situation I hear you've got going for yourself?"

It had been two days since Hope moved over to the guesthouse. She'd only waited until the next morning after her memory had returned because Evie had already been asleep for the night. If not for the baby, Ridge was certain she would have moved over there that very night.

Now here it was halfway through the week. Villanueva's involvement was no longer necessary. He'd sent Ridge some links about the accident that claimed Danny Marks's life, along with his final bill. He'd done everything he could. The protection that Hope needed now would come from having better lawyers than Howard and Petunia had.

Lawyers that Ridge could provide, but only if Hope agreed.

Which she was refusing to do.

"I'm not taking more charity than I already have," she'd told him the evening before. "Soon as I can find a paycheck that doesn't get swallowed up by day care for Evie, I'll start paying you back for everything you've done for me."

No mention whatsoever about the fact that he'd told her he loved her.

And damn sure no response in kind.

When he'd made the suggestion that she didn't *need* to work, he'd immediately recognized his monumental error.

But no amount of apologizing seemed to help.

Now, he wasn't just afraid of not being able to protect her and Evie from her former in-laws, he was half afraid she'd decide she didn't want the use of the guesthouse at all. It wasn't as if it was perfect. Didn't even have an actual stove in it. Just a microwave and a dorm-sized refrigerator.

"What do you do with a stubborn woman, Beau?"

The older man chuckled. "Love 'em anyway."

"Nobody said anything about love."

"Son, you've been in love with that young lady and her baby girl for months."

Ridge squared himself to the table and circled his coffee mug with his hands. He'd never once subscribed to Beau's "free life advice." Aside from consulting him about real estate, which was just good business sense as far as Ridge was concerned. "Was your wife a stubborn woman?" He knew Beau's wife had died quite some time ago. And they'd been married a long, long time.

"She was." Beau's eyes were reflective. "When she needed to be."

Ridge grimaced. "That's real helpful, Beau. Thanks."

"Every relationship is a give-and-take. Problems can get real interesting when you both are taking opposing stands over something at the same time. Otherwise…" He shrugged and glanced at the door when it opened.

The faint smile around his lips returned as they both watched Ridge's mother sail through the doorway.

They weren't alone. Every other person in the place also took note when Wendy entered.

"You have a fine-lookin' mama," Beau murmured under his breath. His gaze followed her to the counter, where she propped an indolent elbow and bestowed her brilliant smile on the barista before tossing back her hair and laughing at something the teenage boy said. She was dressed in winter white, from the skinny turtleneck down to the tall leather boots she had tucked her jeans into.

"Yeah," Ridge said tartly, "and she's not looking for romance. She told me so herself just a few days ago. So, cool your jets, old man."

Beau grinned. He shifted and hooked one arm over the back of his chair as he maintained his attention on Wendy. "I'd be careful about who you're calling old," he warned. "I can still wrestle a steer when the need arises."

"Is that the sum of your life advice today?"

Beau picked up his coffee mug and nodded. "Seems so. Although, I'll add free of charge—" a big offer since the placard on the corner of Beau's regular table at the Daily Grind announced *Free* Life Advice "—that Zane's offer on Nonny's place was with the intent of subdividing it for a housing development."

"Chatelaine needs a housing development?"

"Not now," Beau said. "Down the line? Who knows?"

"You're the local wise man. Aren't you the one who's supposed to know?"

"Chatelaine's not a burgeoning market. It's small, but it's held its own for a lot of years. Not shrinking. Just plodding along. Might be time for some growth to hit. 'Specially with that castle of your mother's bringing in new sets of eyes."

"Where you going with this, Beau?"

The other man squinted slightly as he sipped his coffee. Ridge wasn't sure if it was from the hot drink, from contemplation, or because he was getting a better bead on Ridge's mother's figure.

"Just that the probate judge was an old friend of Nonny Zazlo. He'll know the notion of the family ranch getting chopped into rows for ticky-tacky houses would make him turn over in his grave. If there were a competing offer from someone who intended to continue using the land for ranching…" He squinted and sipped again.

"The last thing I'm thinking about right now is that property," Ridge said under his breath because his mom had straightened from the counter and turned their direction, carrying her tall coffee cup in one hand.

"Sometimes fixing one thing can lead to another thing getting fixed almost all on its own," Beau told him cryptically.

Then he pushed to his feet and swept his Stetson off the table in invitation in the same motion that he practically yanked Ridge's chair out from under him. "Morning, Miz Fortune. You're looking mighty cheerful."

"Beau Weatherly," Wendy greeted. "Just the man I'd hoped to see." She presented her cheek for Ridge's kiss and gracefully sank onto his abruptly vacated chair. Then, setting her boxy leather purse on one corner of the table, she smiled brilliantly at both men. "Ridge." She tsked. "You look like you've been pulled backward through a knothole. When's the last time you shaved?"

He didn't feel self-conscious all that often, but if someone could inspire it, it would be his mother. He rubbed his palm down his scratchy jaw.

"Hope's living in the guesthouse," Beau said, as if it would be news to Wendy.

"I know. And we had a wonderful chat just this morning." Her gaze drifted over Ridge again. "Don't you have somewhere else to be, honey? I thought Arlo and Nash were meeting this morning."

"They are. And there's nothing particularly important that I can contribute," Ridge answered flatly. "Unless we buy more land, we don't have room for more stock. We're running as many cow-calf pairs as we can. Dahlia needs her parcels for her sheep. Jade needs hers for the petting zoo. Status quo is maintained whether I show up to look at Arlo and Nash's weekly charts or not."

Wendy's eyebrows had risen slightly. "Well, I suppose you could take a look at the castle—"

He swore. Then grimaced. "Sorry," he muttered. He usually tried not to swear around his mother. "That's the problem in the first place, Mom. I don't need you to make up another job for me." He exhaled loudly. He was more annoyed with himself than he was with her. "Ignore me. I'll figure it out."

"I've never doubted it," Wendy assured blithely. "Perhaps you could check in on Sabrina. She has a new project on her hands."

Ridge jerked. "That's not some clever way of saying she's having the babies, is it?"

"Good Lord, Ridge. Of course it isn't. Do you think I'd be sitting around here—albeit enjoying some very fine company— if I had two more grandchildren making their entrance to the world?" She looked across at Beau, who had seated himself again across from Wendy.

"Stress," Beau mused. "Does things to a person's reasoning unless they find some outlet."

Ridge shook his head, stomped over to the counter to get a lid for his coffee and left.

He drove back to the ranch and stopped at the petting zoo. But Jade just shook her head when he appeared outside, where she was refilling one of the enormous buckets of feed that dozens of little hands would spread around for the goats and the pigs. "Hope didn't bring Evie this morning," she told him. "She did send me a text message, though, to let me know not to worry."

The only other time that Hope hadn't taken Evie to the zoo had been when her baby was sick.

He turned to go, making his way through the gift shop back to the entrance. The sight of a tall giraffe caught his attention, though. He went back out to catch Jade's eye. "When did the giraffe come in?"

"Yesterday morning. I can't keep too many of them in stock. They take up too much room."

"Not this one," he told her and went back inside the shop again. He purchased the giraffe from the volunteer operating the cash register—he could never keep up with the names of the people who cycled through Jade's place on a regular basis—and maneuvered the stuffed animal into the back of his SUV. He had to let the giraffe's head stick out the window because it was so tall, which earned a few amused looks when he drove out of the parking lot and turned toward his place.

He doubted that he'd find Hope and Evie inside the house. Even though he'd told her she could use the kitchen in the main house, she hadn't done so yet. He wandered down through "her" wing.

The nursery looked painfully empty without Evie's crib. The rocking chair sat forlornly in the corner. The other toys and stuffed animals were gone, as were the lithographs from the wall.

He walked through the bathroom to Hope's bedroom on the other side.

There wasn't a single thing left to say she'd ever occupied the place. Not even a strand of auburn hair.

Terralee was nothing if not efficient.

He went back outside and wrestled the giraffe out of the back. It wasn't that the animal was particularly heavy, but it was as tall as Ridge. He grabbed it around its brown and yellow torso and lifted it off the ground to carry around to the guesthouse.

The door of which was locked.

He set the giraffe on the porch and looked through the windows, but the wood blinds were angled so that all he could see inside was a few inches of sun-dappled floor.

He tried the doorknob again. Just to be doubly certain it was locked.

Hope didn't have any money. The golf cart was parked in its usual spot off to the side of his house. He texted his mom.

Where was it that you talked to Hope this morning?

But his mother didn't reply. No dancing dots even to indicate that she was in the process of it.

The weather was calling for rain again, so he took the giraffe back over to his house and left it inside the foyer. Then he got in his SUV and headed back down the drive.

Stopping to open and close the gate again was a pain, but until he fixed the opener, there wasn't anything he could do about it.

He aimed the SUV toward the ranch headquarters and

called Evie's pediatrician office along the way. No, they hadn't made an appointment that morning to see the baby.

It was something at least.

Gravel spun under his tires when he turned off to the headquarters. His mood was even darker as he spotted Zane standing in front of the massive photocopier. Ridge stopped next to him. "Tract housing, Zane? That's what you have in mind for the Zazlo spread?"

Zane raised his eyebrows, his expression mild. "It's one possibility," he said. He took a sheaf of papers from the copier bin and dumped them in Ridge's surprised hands. "Take those for Hope."

Frowning, he looked down at the stack of colorful sheets in his hands. Boot Camp for Dads!

"What the hell are these?"

Zane shrugged. "What it says. Boot camp for dads. Sabrina asked me to copy 'em so I copied. I was going to drop them off at your place, but now I don't have to and—" he looked at his watch "—I'm late for a meeting." He lifted his hand and strode away.

Ridge turned to head toward Sabrina's office. He got halfway there when Nash stuck his head out of his office. "I thought I heard your voice," he greeted. "You missed our meeting this morning."

"I missed your and Arlo's meeting," Ridge corrected, but he stopped in front of Nash, who'd retreated back into his office. "Here." He slapped down a half dozen of the flyers on his brother's desk. Nash was a new dad. He could use pointers just as much as anyone.

"What're those?"

He regurgitated the brief exchange he'd just had with Zane. "Talk to Sabrina if you have questions."

Nash showed about as much interest as Ridge felt and

pushed the flyers to one side. He took a folder from his desk and extended it. "Take a look. It's the budget for the next fiscal year. Want your take on it before we finalize it."

"I've already told you what I thought. We can't expand without acquiring more land."

Nash flicked his fingers. "And we listened. Stop thinking we never do, Ridge." His phone pinged, and after a glance, he immediately answered. "Imani."

Ridge could see the change in his brother's expression just from saying the woman's name, and he wondered if he looked as besotted where Hope was concerned.

Probably.

Did it bother him?

Not in the least.

He just wished he could *find* her. He left Nash's office and went down to Arlo's. His brother didn't work there all the time since he had his own business to take care of, but he used his office more often than Ridge did. He glanced in. Arlo was leaning back in his chair, his ankles crossed atop his desk. He was talking on the phone. Obviously a business call.

Ridge left him a few flyers, too. Aviva was a toddler already, but the flyer didn't specify any particular age of kids as a focus for the boot camp.

Finally, he went down to Sabrina's office.

And sitting right there, her head bent over a bunch of forms on the desk, was Hope.

His heartbeat jerked around a little as he stood there watching her unawares. Evie was sitting in her stroller next to Hope's chair, and she spotted him, though, and squealed, stretching out her hands, her fingers opening and closing.

Hope looked up then, and her periwinkle gaze crashed into his.

"Where's Sabrina?" he asked thickly.

"Ladies' room."

He dropped the flyers on the desk next to the papers that Hope had been poring over and plucked Evie out of the stroller. "I went looking for you," he said. "I was a little worried when I didn't find you." He buzzed Evie's neck, and she gave a satisfyingly joyful belly laugh. At least one of his ladies was still happy with him.

"I left a note on the counter in the kitchen where I'd be."

He hadn't gone *into* the kitchen.

"Your mom offered me a job," she said. She lifted the paper, and he realized it was an employment application.

"Doing what?"

She frowned slightly at his tone. "Does it matter?"

He exhaled. Nuzzled the other side of Evie's neck until he earned another belly laugh. Listening to her laugh was the best de-stressor that he could think of.

While she was still chortling, he propped his hip on the corner of Sabrina's desk. "It doesn't matter," he said more reasonably. "Whatever it is, I know you'll be great at it."

Her lashes swept down but not quickly enough to hide the gleam of pleasure. "She wants me to open a day care center to serve the children of all the ranch workers," she told him.

"Are there that many?"

"Ten so far on the waiting list. I happen to know that Chatelaine Hills doesn't have a single day care center."

"Probably a lot of private nannies," he said.

"Yes, but—" she lifted her index finger "—sometimes that is by necessity because there aren't any other options. And particularly affordable options. But, anyway, I wasn't thinking so much about the people who can afford to live in the fancy houses out here as the workers, who more likely live in Chatelaine where it's more affordable and have to drive out here to the lake to make a living. With a good childcare center in the area where they work—"

"You don't have to sell me on this, Hope. I think it's a great idea. But starting small with just the ranch kids isn't a bad thing."

"I know. And that's what I'll do. I have to hire enough staff to meet the local regulations and find a facility that—"

She broke off when Sabrina waddled back into the office, her hands pressed against her back as if she needed a counterweight for her belly.

Ridge swung her chair around for her to sit. He'd sort of been joking earlier about her having the babies, but now he wasn't so sure. "You okay there, sis?"

"Just experiencing the joy of gestating," Sabrina assured breathlessly. She rolled her chair closer to the desk, which wasn't very close at all, and reached for one of her trusty perfectly pointed pencils. "If you haven't seen Nash, he has a copy of the proposed budget for you."

"I've got it." He'd flattened it into a cylinder and stuck it in his back pocket. He actually had some interest in reading it now that he knew about the day care thing. "Did you know your fiancé's planning to build tract houses in Chatelaine? Out near the water tower?"

"If you have a problem with Zane's business, talk to Zane."

"I don't have a problem with it—"

"Zane is buying the Zazlo property?"

He looked at Hope. "That's what I hear."

She frowned slightly. "I'm sorry."

Sabrina's gaze was bouncing between them. "What's going on here?" she said slowly. Suspiciously.

Ridge grimaced. He set Evie back into the stroller and waggled a squishy pink octopus in front of her. She grabbed at it and greedily shoved one of the legs into her mouth. "I was considering buying it," he admitted.

"Kind of far for an expansion of the ranch, isn't it?"

"I wasn't thinking of it as an expansion. I was thinking of it as something *I* would run. Me."

Comprehension dawned on his sister's face. "Oh." She winced slightly and rubbed a soothing hand over one side of her belly. "Foot, I think. Under the ribs." She leaned back in her chair. "You need to tell Mom," she said bluntly.

"How do you know I haven't?"

Sabrina gave him a look.

"I know I need to," he muttered. "I came close this morning, too." Even though Beau knew more about Ridge's plans than anyone—save Hope—he hadn't felt like having that discussion with his mother in front of the other man.

"Excuse me," a timid voice from the doorway interrupted them, and they all looked around to see the mousy receptionist who sometimes filled in when the regular woman was off. Miriam. Marjorie. Something like that. "There's someone here to see Miss—er—Mrs. Marks."

Hope's gaze flew to Ridge's. Her alarm was plain.

"Who?" Ridge's question was sharp.

"Uh. I—" The girl looked uncertain. "I didn't ask his name. He's older, though. Almost bald. Should I go—"

"It's fine, Mariah," Sabrina said. "Thank you."

At least he'd been close on the woman's name. He didn't take his attention from Hope. "I'll go see—"

Despite her obvious alarm, annoyance flickered in the blue depths. "No." She placed her pen carefully on top of the employment form she'd been completing.

There was only one nearly bald older man who'd be seeking Hope out from anywhere, and they all knew it.

"Would you keep Evie back here for me?"

Every instinct he possessed wanted to argue. Only the sudden warning tug on the back of his shirt by his sister reminded him to tread cautiously. Acquiescing, he picked Evie back up from the stroller. She batted him on the head with her octopus. "I'm two seconds away," he told Hope, following her out of the office.

She nodded. She was wearing another bright sweater—this one red—over leggings, and she smoothed the hem as she walked away from him.

Ridge pressed his forehead against Evie's. There was no way in hell he was going to let anyone take her away from Hope.

Sabrina tugged his shirt again. "Look."

He turned to see her holding a monitor almost like the ones that he'd gotten around the house for Evie. It showed a color image of the reception area. "I got this because it was simpler than having to haul myself to my feet and see who was here every time I'm working alone," she explained. "Zane's idea."

The camera showed the top of Mariah's head as she returned to her desk, but it was mostly focused on the entry. His chest ached as he watched Hope cross in and out of the camera's view. Sabrina nudged the control on the camera and followed after Hope.

The guy sitting in one of the chairs was lanky. Definitely balding.

And definitely *not* Howard Marks.

"Holly Marks?" His voice was loud through the monitor.
Hope nodded.

Ridge saw it coming then. And there wasn't a thing he could do about it.

The man extended an envelope, and Hope automatically reached out and took it.

"Consider yourself served," he said with a smirk of satisfaction. Then he walked briskly out of the door.

Ridge met Sabrina's eyes. "Damn," she murmured.

And then some.

"She has a point. Meeting her husband's parents face-to-face for a discussion might defuse the situation. Keep the lawyers out of it. Maybe they can come to a resolution without Hope ever needing to return to Nashville next month for that subpoena."

Ridge glared at Beau, not really sure why the man was there for what Ridge considered a private family matter, but he'd arrived along with Wendy when Sabrina had sent out her bat-signal text to the family and that was that.

"Meeting with Howard and Petunia isn't what I have a problem with," he said now, pacing across the empty break room. Nash had sent everyone home so they could have the building to themselves. He glanced at Hope, who sat at one of the tables scattered around the utilitarian room. "It's meeting with them *alone*," he clarified pointedly.

Her lips tightened and her chin lifted slightly. His mother was seated next to her. She was bouncing Evie slightly on her lap. "This is Hope's decision," she said.

Ridge's nerves tightened. "You agree with her, Mom? Really? You think this is the way to fix—"

Hope suddenly stood. "I'm sorry. Would you all excuse us for a sec?" She wrapped her hand around Ridge's forearm, her fingertips digging.

He followed her out of the room and closed the door to the break room. But that wasn't far enough evidently, because she kept walking, dragging him after her.

All the way outside the building.

Fitting that the clouds were dark as tar and a wind had kicked up.

She let go and turned on him. Her hair lifted around her shoulders. "I don't need you to *fix* me." Her voice shook. "I thought you understood that!"

What he understood was that—once again—what he wanted most in this world was just out of his grasp. "I didn't say fix *you*. I meant this fu—" He ground his teeth together. "This situation," he said finally. "This is how we work, Hope. This family. We do it together."

"Oh, like you're doing Mr. Rancherman together with them," she scoffed. "You won't even tell your mother that you want a ranch of your own. How is that *together*?"

Sometimes he was slow to the party. "Picking a fight with me isn't going to change my mind. Meet Howard and Petunia if you think it's what you need to do. But for God's sake, don't do it all on your own, Hope. You don't need—"

"My name is Holly," she yelled. *"Holly!"*

It felt like a punch to his kidneys.

It hadn't been so long ago that she'd told him she'd wished her name was Hope for real.

"Right," he said. "I'm sorry."

Her shoulders sagged. "I'm sorry! Try to understand, Ridge. Getting my memory back is…hard."

"I know."

"No! You don't know. You can't possibly. You can sympathize, but you can't know." Her hair whipped across her face, and she pushed at it, futilely. "I need to figure out who I am. Who I…who I *want* to be. And I… I can't do that." Her voice thickened. Sounded choked. "I can't do that with you always right there. Ready to save the day when I screw it up."

"You're not screwing up anything."

"I'm screwing up *us*!" She pulled her hair back from her

face again, and he could see the tears in her eyes. "You love *Hope*," she said thickly. "The person you found unconscious in your barn. The person you've been playing house with. Evie's mom, who takes her to the petting zoo and steals flowers from people's gardens to put in jars."

His mother was right, he thought.

Happiness slipped through a person's fingers like sand.

"That's *you*," he ground out. But until she could merge her past with her present, he could finally see that no amount of trying on his part would convince her of anything.

He'd known it all along. That she'd break his heart.

Strange that he hadn't been more prepared.

"Stay in the guesthouse as long as you need," he said. "I'll stay out of your way. I'd just like to—" he stared into the wind "—to see Evie now and then."

She sniffled. Wiped the tears with the backs of her hands. "Of course. Evie loves you."

But her mother didn't.

He wiped a raindrop from his cheek.

Maybe it was a raindrop.

Maybe not.

"I appreciate that—" he steeled himself "—Holly."

Then he did the only thing left to do.

He turned and walked away.

Chapter Fifteen

"**B**ut you *have* to come," Sabrina said. She waved her hand at the lovely watercolor dress that was hanging on the closet door of the guesthouse. "That dress deserves to see a wedding. And Javier and Belinda's grandson is the first one on the list for Fortunate Futures. You can't *not* go!"

Despite the misery that she'd felt ever since Ridge had called her Holly the week before, she couldn't help smiling a little. "We haven't decided on Fortunate Futures as the name for the day care," she reminded Sabrina.

"It's better than Little Darlings or Precious Footsteps." At the first planning meeting for Wendy Fortune's latest business brainchild, both names had been tossed into the hat along with Fortunate Futures and a half dozen more. "It's too bad that we couldn't make use of the space at the castle." Sabrina twitched the fabric of the watercolor dress, and it seemed to shimmer slightly in the sunlight angling through the window.

It was the window that faced directly at Ridge's house, and Holly had taken to keeping the blinds closed. Sabrina had opened them, though.

Holly would have to close them again later.

It was just easier. Stave off temptation and not find herself wallowing at the window, hoping for some fleeting glance of him coming or going.

The only times she had seen him since that awful day the week before were when she took Evie to the petting zoo.

He'd give her a polite nod, take over the stroller and go off with her daughter for a brief period. Proof that he'd meant what he said about keeping his distance, it was always Jade who brought Evie and the stroller back to Hope.

She shook her head. She was worse than all of them.

Holly.

Her gaze landed on the giraffe that had appeared on their doorstep a few days ago, and she looked away again.

She knew things were over for her and Ridge. Had known it when she'd screamed at him like a banshee and he'd used her name. Her *real* name.

For him, Hope was no more. She'd seen it in his eyes.

But things weren't over for Evie and Ridge.

Hope—*dammit*—Holly wasn't sure how she'd be able to stand it.

"The castle is a little far from the ranch," she reminded his sister a little belatedly. "We need a location that is readily accessible for the parents who'll be using the center."

"I know." Sabrina rubbed her back and paced across the small room. "This place isn't even half the size of the guesthouse at Nash's," she said. "What gives with that?"

Holly lifted her shoulder. "Complain to the builder I guess." She knew what Sabrina was really doing there. Trying to keep her mind off the looming meeting that she was having with Howard and Petunia that afternoon. In an effort to find a neutral location, they'd settled on one of the private meeting rooms at the LC Club.

She'd given in on having legal assistance from the Fortunes. Wendy had talked her around on that. So it had been a kindly bespectacled man named Luther Cook who'd reached out to the Markses' lawyer to arrange the meeting, during which both lawyers would remain outside the room. If one was needed to intervene, both would.

Her phone pinged softly, and she picked it up to see the image of Aviva and Evie playing together with a stack of blocks and dolls. Arlo's fiancée, Carrie, had offered to keep Evie, and she'd been providing reassuring messages and pics throughout the day.

"I suppose we should go," Sabrina finally said. She was in charge of delivering Holly to the LC Club.

Holly chewed the inside of her lip and nodded. She brushed her hands down the front of the black slacks she was wearing with a white blouse and black jacket.

"Sometimes a suit is called for, honey," Wendy had said when she'd delivered it the day before. "Whenever I'm feeling nervous, a little Prada or Chanel always helps."

Thankfully, the label inside the garments had been much more mainstream or she would have been too intimidated to wear them.

Holly went into the bathroom long enough to make sure her hair was still smoothed back in a neat ponytail and that her mascara hadn't smeared. She looked like she was on her way to a job interview, quite frankly.

But the suit did make her feel like she walked a little taller. She picked up the leather purse that Wendy had loaned her and opened the door.

Despite herself, she couldn't help looking over at Ridge's house when she opened her umbrella and followed Sabrina to her SUV. Neither his Escalade nor the rusty old pickup were there. Whatever that was supposed to mean.

The umbrella collapsed, she bit back a sigh and fastened her seat belt, closing her eyes. Tried a few of the breathing and visualization tips she'd gotten from the therapist she'd seen at the beginning of the week. She'd already made the appointment before her memory had returned. When she'd gotten the text message reminder about the appointment, she'd decided to go.

Couldn't do any more harm than she'd already done all on her own.

Syrie Landers had proved to be surprisingly down to earth and practical. None of the woo-woo stuff Holly remembered from some of the social workers who'd passed through her youth. "Small steps," she'd told Holly. "Every journey starts with one step. Remember that."

When she opened her eyes again, Sabrina was pulling into a parking spot at the LC Club. The lot wasn't even half-full. Rainy Thursday afternoons evidently weren't prime time. Sabrina handed her the compact umbrella. "I'll be waiting right here. Luther should have already arrived."

She nodded. "If I forget to tell you later—"

Sabrina squeezed her hand. "I know." Her eyes looked a little damp. "Now, go get 'em."

Holly opened the umbrella and quickly crossed to the entrance. A slender girl in a knee-length sheath dress pointed out the way, and a few minutes later, she was greeting Luther, who was sitting in a chair outside a closed door. He introduced her to the stoic-faced woman who occupied the chair on the other side of the door. "Wanda Ledbetter," he said.

Holly shook her hand. She'd be damned if she'd say "pleased to meet you," since she was anything but. "I appreciate you taking the time today," she settled on.

Then she steeled herself, pushed open the door and went inside. "Hello, Howard." She looked at Petunia sitting next to him at the end of a long table that could have sat sixteen. "Petunia."

She could see Danny's mother looking behind her, as if she expected the door to open again.

"I didn't bring Evie, if that's what you were hoping for. I'm certain your attorney informed you that I would be alone."

Petunia's lips tightened. She whispered something to Howard.

Holly deliberately uncurled her fingers from fisting. She walked over to the table. Pulled out the chair at the end and sat with her hands folded on top of the table in front of her. The power position. She'd seen Wendy Fortune do it many times now. "Thank you for coming."

Petunia's eyes flashed. "As if you gave us a choice?"

"You still have a choice," Holly said. "No one is forcing you to be here. You could have chosen to wait until next month at the courthouse in Nashville. You're the ones bringing a suit against me to take custody of my child."

"*Danny's* child," Petunia said harshly.

"Yes," Holly agreed evenly. "And Danny is gone. Sadly, he's never going to know what a beautiful girl we created."

"He's *gone* because of you."

Howard put a calming hand on Petunia's. "You agreed," he said under his breath, but not so much so that Holly couldn't hear.

Petunia looked angry, but she clamped her lips together.

Funny. But Holly had never realized how much more Danny had resembled her than he had Howard. She'd always thought he'd looked more like his dad.

"How *is* Evie?" Howard asked gruffly.

"She's fine. She's starting to talk some. Crawls like a fiend." She leaned down and pulled the manila envelope from the purse. Then stood and carried the envelope down to him. "She loves her bath time and being outdoors." She set the envelope on the table near Howard and returned to her seat. "She's a good eater and a good sleeper and she's the light of my life. And—" she folded her hands again and hoped that her white knuckles weren't visible from their end of the table "—she deserves to have a relationship with her grandparents."

"*We* should be raising her," Petunia said, obviously striving to keep herself in check.

"Why? Because you think I don't know the way families should behave? That somehow, because I was pretty much raised in the foster care system my whole life, I lack something that *you* possess?"

"Danny told us about your past."

"My past that could be a lot worse than it was? I never did drugs. I could have. The opportunity was there almost every day of my life. I graduated from high school. Earned a scholarship to get a child development degree. How about you, Petunia? What's your *past* like?" She squeezed her hands tighter, counting in her head until her racing heart slowed back down again.

"If that's some sort of threat—"

"You beat Danny once with a pair of scissors," she said quietly. "He had a scar on his shoulder from it."

"Enough," Howard said heavily. "Nobody's life looks perfect when you shine a magnifying glass over it. Including Danny's." He'd slid the photographs out from the envelope, and they were spread across the table in front of him. She saw the way his fingers trembled a little as he touched the most recent one of Evie, with her hair tied up in a tiny ponytail on the top of her head while she reached out to pet one of Jade's bearded goats. "She looks like you," he said.

"I think she's beautiful, so I'll take that as a compliment."

"Howard, this is a waste of time," his wife snapped.

"If you don't behave yourself, Pet, you can sit outside with that termagant of a lawyer you hired."

Holly sank her teeth into her tongue to keep from reacting.

Howard looked at Holly. "I'm sixty-five years old," he said. "By the time Evie's school-age, I—*we*—" he gave his wife a pointed look "—will be seventy. When you say you want Evie to have a relationship with us, what does that mean?"

"Not having *had* grandparents," Holly said carefully, "I can only say that I think it means extra hugs. Extra love. Phone calls just to chatter together. Trips to a zoo. Maybe an overnight now and then." She lifted her palms. "It means what it needs to mean. But it doesn't mean usurping my role as her *mother*."

"I'm telling you, Howard—"

"I warned you, Pet." He gave his wife a look. "I let you spoil Danny his entire life, and he became an unhappy, discontented adult who'd sooner lie to us about the color of the sky than tell the truth. And I bear just as much blame as you for not stopping it when I had the chance.

"Now." Howard turned back to Holly. "Let's cut to the chase, shall we?"

She realized her mouth had dropped open and quickly shut it. She nodded once. "Let's."

"Still in there, I take it." Ridge stood outside of his sister's SUV, his shoulders hunched against the damp.

"Yeah." Sabrina eyed him. "You could sit inside you know. The LC Club. My car. Either would be better than standing out in the rain."

"I don't want to chance her knowing I'm here."

She quirked a brow. "Taking the distance thing a little far, don't you think?"

"I'm giving her what she wants."

"Right now, Hope doesn't know *what* she wants. Zane called it, you know. Said she's in survival mode. Just trying to get through. He'd felt that way when he'd ended up being responsible for raising his siblings. It won't last forever."

"It's been almost two hours. Let me know what happens." He flipped his collar up and angled across the large parking lot. He'd parked around the block in the lot for a small strip of medical offices.

Ridge was soaked through by the time he reached the Escalade. The only thing he had to dry himself with was a forgotten blanket of Evie's. He ran it over his face and head and sat there for another hour with the pink fabric twisting in his hands before he got a text from Sabrina.

No words. Just a thumbs-up.

He lowered his head and breathed fully for the first time in days.

Chapter Sixteen

Holly stood outside of the town hall building and wondered what she was doing there.

Javier and Belinda Mendes would have plenty of people present to celebrate their latest nuptials without Holly being there.

A thin man wearing a cowboy hat and dress boots brushed past her and pulled open the heavy door. "Going inside?"

She brushed her hands down the sides of the watercolor dress. Her cell phone was tucked in one of the hidden side pockets. A small jeweler's box was in the other.

Holly knew what she was doing there.

She'd left Evie in Howard's care back at the guesthouse. Her former father-in-law had told her he'd sent Petunia back home to Nashville the morning after they'd met.

She wasn't sure she would have left her baby with him if Petunia had still been there.

Yes, they'd all agreed to some general terms.

But Holly would believe Petunia could refrain from trying to take over again when she saw it.

Howard, though? He'd been a lot more convincing.

She only needed to stay long enough to get through the wedding ceremony. Maintain her self-control long enough to give Ridge back the pendant. She could wait until she got back to the guesthouse before falling apart and then some-how summoning the willpower to do everything else that needed doing.

Finding a more permanent place to live was at the head of the list.

She obviously couldn't remain in Ridge's guesthouse.

Another person brushed past her, heels clicking loudly on the floor tile and clearly following one of the signs with the word *wedding* flowing in elegant script across the board.

She followed, too, and caught her breath a little in pure feminine appreciation when she slipped into the back of the event room. Clearly, practice made perfect where the Mendeses' wedding decor was concerned. Her intention of remaining in the back of the room went by the wayside when Jade and Heath came in right after her. Jade wrapped her hands around Holly's wrist and pulled her down the aisle between the seats to the bunch of chairs surprisingly near the front that were still vacant.

If she'd had more of her wits about her, she would have realized she'd let Jade shuffle her into the seat right behind Ridge.

He looked over his shoulder at her. Then his sister.

Jade immediately shuffled one seat over, making room for Ridge, who made Holly gape when he stepped right over the back of the pretty white folding chair to take the seat next to her.

His hand closed around hers almost the way that Jade's had, except *his* touch made her tremble, and when he pressed his thumb against her pulse, she was left wondering if it was hers that thumped so hard, or his.

"Stay," he said. "The music's already starting."

And it was. Amid the lovely swags of white fabric and

the clusters of palest pink roses, the string trio seated in the corner of the room had begun the traditional wedding march.

A smiling man wearing a black suit moved to the center at the head of the aisle and opened a Bible. He was obviously the officiant.

Sabrina, who was sitting in the row behind Holly, leaned forward as they stood in preparation for the "mystery" bride to enter. "Pool's up to two hundred bucks," she whispered.

Despite everything, Holly had to bite back a smile. Far as she was concerned, Sabrina still had the inside track, knowing about the Mendeses' vacation requests.

The music reached a crescendo, and the doors at the back of the room opened again. She craned her neck to see, but all she got was a glimpse of a flowing champagne-hued gown.

All around her, though, she heard gasps.

"I'll be—"

"*No* way!"

"Ssh!" Jade was trying to hush her siblings without success.

"Holy sh—" Ridge cut off his stunned reaction when Holly hastily poked him in the side before snatching back her hand and clasping it at her waist.

And then she, too, could just stare as the bridal couple came level with their row.

Wendy Fortune, radiant in silk and lace and carrying an elegantly simple bouquet of long-stem roses, smiled at them and gave a little wink before she continued forward on the arm of a very handsome-looking Beau Weatherly.

Holly looked at the faces around her.

To say they all looked shocked was putting it mildly.

"Please be seated," the officiant invited, and there was a general shuffling in the room as the music trailed away and the guests sat.

And watched in dumbfounded consensus as Wendy Windham Fortune became Mrs. Beau Weatherly.

Later, of course, it all made sense.

The mysterious requests for a favorite photograph as a gift. For a meaningful quotation.

After the ceremony, Holly, still unable to extricate herself from the throng of Ridge and his siblings, found herself sitting in the adjacent room that had been decorated just as beautifully for the reception. The string trio had been replaced by a small live band, and servers were moving in and around the tables offering food and drink while the bride and groom took command of the dance floor in a wholly *un*traditional tango that left Wendy's sons looking up at the ceiling and down at the floor and Wendy's daughters muffling their delight behind their hands.

The rest of the guests all stood up with a whooping holler when the dance concluded with Beau leaning Wendy over in a swoon-worthy dip.

Then the radiant bride rose and kissed her new husband and spontaneously tossed the long-stem rose bouquet she'd been holding all the while.

It sailed through the air and landed squarely in Ridge's lap.

He looked chagrined and after a moment handed the bouquet to Holly.

Her face felt on fire. She wanted to push it away but she also didn't want to make a scene. She ended up setting the beautiful stems in the center of the table. "We'll all enjoy them," she said.

Fortunately, Wendy and Beau were beckoning others to join them on the dance floor, and amid the commotion, Holly was able to finally escape.

She made it as far as the bathroom down the hall before

the tears came. She closed herself in a stall and cried until she couldn't cry any more.

She cried for the naive girl who'd married for all the right reasons but still hadn't found happiness. Mostly, she cried for the Hope she'd never really been. She cried until someone tapped on the door. "Y'alright in there, hon?"

"Fine," she said thickly. And waited until the woman had flushed and washed and left again.

She left the stall and shook her head at her reflection. Eyes swollen. Nose red.

"Lovely," she muttered.

"You are." Ridge stepped into the room and closed the door.

Her heart climbed into her throat. "You can't be in here."

"And yet—" he spread his arms, looking ridiculously handsome in his perfectly tailored black suit and caramel-colored silk T-shirt "—I *am* in here." As if to drive the point, he flipped the lock on the door.

She pressed her hands behind her against the marble counter. The wedding decor had continued even into the bathroom, she realized. A vase of glorious roses sat next to the sink, and in the little sitting area, the bench was draped with oyster-colored satin.

"Sabrina told me you left Evie with Howard?"

She lifted her chin slightly. "Yes. I'm sure you think that was a bad idea."

"I think it was the *only* idea." He stepped closer. "He's Evie's grandfather. Villanueva did a check on him. Seems to be a stand-up guy except for his taste in a wife."

"He sent her back to Nashville."

"I heard." He took another step toward her.

She sidled around him, almost surprised that he let her reverse their positions. Only, once she'd succeeded, she didn't really know what to do next. The music from the reception was still perfectly audible—a painfully romantic "Someone Like You."

She nervously shoved her hands into her pockets. She could unlock the door. Leave.

Why didn't she?

"The giraffe is huge," she said abruptly.

His hooded gaze was serious. But his beautiful mouth smiled slightly. "It was huge. Head stuck out the window like a happy dog when I drove it home."

She pressed her lips together. The image in her head was priceless. "Evie loves it," she managed after a moment.

Her fingers toyed with the jeweler's box.

The reason she'd come to what she'd thought would be a mildly interesting wedding. "Quite the surprise from your mom and Beau."

"Quite. Apparently, they've been involved all along. Kept it quiet at first because it was so soon after my father died. Then kept it quiet longer because..." He shrugged. "Who knows? My mother is nothing if not surprising."

"You *never* suspected?"

He shook his head. "Probably should have. But I've had a pretty big distraction of my own."

She felt her skin flush and realized she'd retreated again only because the back of her knees bumped the satin-covered bench, and she sat with an inelegant plop. "You don't have to worry about distractions anymore," she said. "So you can move on to Oklahoma or...or wherever and—"

"I'm not going to Oklahoma or any other wherever."

"I thought Zane was buying the Zazlo property."

"Got it right that time," he murmured. "He is. At least that was the plan last I heard." He stepped closer.

She was having the hardest time breathing normally.

Maybe she was allergic to roses and had never known it before. She fastened her hands around the jewelry box and yanked it from her pocket. She stuck out her hand, the box between them. As if it would ward him off or something. "You need to take this back."

He didn't reach for it.

She thumbed the box lid. Pushed it open. The beautiful key pendant nestled among the velvet exactly where it had been the day he'd given it to her. "It was your Christmas gift to me."

"I know what it is." His deep brown gaze had hers ensnared, and she couldn't seem to look away to save her life. "It was a gift, Holly."

The name was like a nail in a coffin. How could she not have known that?

"It's too much."

"If you don't want it, sell it. Start Evie's college fund or put a down payment on a car."

"I could never—"

"What? Sell something that has value but is otherwise meaningless?"

"It's *not* meaningless!"

His eyebrow peaked. "You've never worn it. I assumed you didn't care for it."

"It's from you. Of course I cared for it." The words felt wrenched out of her. "I loved it just like I lo—"

His eyebrow went up another millimeter.

She swiped her face, looking away from him. There was a window above the locked door. A little cascade of ivory and a rosebud was fastened in the corner.

Wendy didn't miss a detail.

Her hand was shaking. She finally lowered it to her lap. "Why did you change your mind about leaving?" She thumbed the lid down on the blue box. "Realize you don't have to go anywhere to invent your next gizmo?"

"I don't want to go any place where *you* are not," he said evenly.

She trembled. "You don't mean that."

"One of these days—" he went down on one knee next to the bench "—you're going to get tired of telling me I don't mean what I very sincerely do." He opened the box and extracted the pendant.

It swung from the fine chain, glittering gently.

"The key is to my heart." His voice was suddenly gruff. "I thought it was a pretty obvious symbol. And you didn't want it." His fingers looked too big to work the tiny, delicate clasp, but he succeeded anyway. He leaned closer to her, bringing with him the scent that had always been faintly heady. Reaching behind her neck, he fastened the necklace, then trailed his fingers down the length of the chain to the pendant that nestled right above her heart.

"But like it or not, it's yours." His fingers went from the pendant to tuck beneath her chin. "I told you before, Holly. You are my *hope*."

Tears sprang to her eyes.

"You are everything I want in this life. You and Evie. And I am not going to go *anywhere* unless you're by my side. Since you're here, that means I'll be here, too." His gaze roved restlessly over her face. He lightly brushed his thumb over her lip.

She could hardly breathe, waiting almost desperately for his head to lower. To feel his kiss again.

His hand fell away.

He pushed to his feet.

"I know you're not ready. But that doesn't change the way I feel. I want to marry you. I want to give Evie my name and a passel of little brothers and sisters to boss around. And if you're never ready?" His lips twisted ruefully. Sadly. "Holly." He flipped the lock and pulled the door open. "Gangreenia Crudbucket," he added. "I'll still love you until there's no more me left."

Then he excused himself and sidled past the line of women that had formed outside of the door.

"So romantic," the first to rush inside gushed. She slammed herself inside a stall.

Another woman followed. "Honey, if you don't want him, I do."

Holly pushed to her feet. "Sorry," she said thickly. "He's taken."

She looked up and down the hall for him but didn't see him. There were so many wedding guests milling about and the music was loud enough that when she called his name, her voice was just swallowed in the noise.

She hurried to the main staircase and looked down. Just in case.

The only person at the base of the stairs was the security guard, leaning against his post and tapping his highly polished boot in time to the music.

She whirled on her heel and hurried back to the reception hall, working her way through the tables and the servers still bearing more food. More wine. Champagne. Cocktails.

She grabbed a sparkling flute as one passed by her and gulped down half.

And then she spotted him.

On the dance floor, doing a very sedate waltz with a woman who looked old enough to be his grandmother.

She left the unfinished champagne on a table and crossed the dance floor. She tapped the woman's brocade-covered shoulder. "May I cut in?"

The woman had snapping black eyes. "If I were a few years younger," she quipped, "I'd tell you no way. But I've got a mile-high slice of wedding cake waiting at my table along with a double bourbon, so." She grinned and surrendered her spot.

And suddenly, Holly's confidence wavered.

She stared up into Ridge's beautiful eyes. The eyes that had never once wavered in kindness. In caring.

In love.

He stood there, hands waiting for her while the dancers moved around them.

Take a breath, she thought. Every worthwhile journey started with just one step.

"Hi," she said, feeling giddy happiness start to swell inside her. This time, she knew whatever was to come, she wouldn't be alone.

Ridge loved her.

And she loved him.

She stuck out her hand as if they were meeting for the first time. "Call me Hope."

He closed his hand around hers. "For the rest of our lives," he said.

Her eyes filled again. But there was no grief. No pain. Only joy. "I love you." She cleared her throat. "For the rest of our lives."

His smile was slow. He drew her against him so closely she couldn't tell his heartbeat from hers.

And they danced.

Across the room, Beau pressed his lips against his bride's temple while they watched her youngest son circle the dance floor with his beloved. "I told you it would work out," he said.

Wendy leaned against him. How quickly and how easily

he'd become her strength. Her roots. "You did," she said a little tearfully. "I was so afraid he would want to go."

"He still might."

"But they'll go with him. He'll have that."

"Yes. And he'll always come back home."

She sighed and turned into his arms, looping her hands around his neck. "Have I told you how handsome you look today? The suit is *very* sexy." She tucked her tongue lightly between her teeth for a moment. "But I happen to know what's underneath is even better."

"Are you propositioning me, Mrs. Weatherly?"

"Every chance I get, Mr. Weatherly."

He looked over her shoulder at the satin-draped table of cards and gifts that people had brought, even though their deliberately cryptic invitation to all their guests had plainly stated that the only gift desired was the invitee's presence. "Maybe we should glance through some of that stuff," he said. "Because darlin', once we start our consummating it's going to be a long while before you're interested in doing anything else."

Wendy's laugh came from her very soul. It was the first thing that had attracted her to Beau. His ability to make her genuinely, truly laugh. Life had given them a second chance together, and they were both grabbing on with ten fingers and ten toes each. "Consummating," she mimicked his drawl. "As if you're some backwoods moonshiner hitchin' his wife."

"Don't knock a good moonshine."

She laughed again and swept up a handful of the cards. Around his shoulder she could see that all of her children were on the dance floor. Even Sabrina. "I hope she doesn't overdo it," she murmured. Much as she loved them, she didn't want to cut short the *consummating* for an emergency trip to the delivery room. "Here." She handed Beau a few cards. "We'll open these and then—" She batted her eyes at him.

He tore open the first of the cards with almost indecent haste. "Congratulations to the happy couple," he read. "From the mayor." He tossed it aside and tore open the next. It contained a similar sentiment. "Pretty hard for people to be personal when they don't know who they're sending the card to in the first place."

"Very true. Look at this one." Wendy was wagging a gold rimmed card that she'd pulled from its heavy, unmarked envelope. "A weekend awaits you as our guest at the Fortune's Gold Guest Ranch," she read. She turned the fancy white card over. The printing on the other side was in gold. "Gift of Fortune," she said. She tapped the card against her chin. "Interesting."

"Fortune's Gold is hours away," Beau remarked. "The guest ranch there's pretty famous." He tugged everything out of her hand and tossed it all aside before drawing her to his feet. "Wouldn't be the worst place to spend a weekend." He kissed her lips. "Probably find some random connection to more of your wild and crazy family."

"We're not wild and crazy," she defended. "We're—"

"Perfectly unique," he assured. Then he wrapped his arm around her waist. The band had struck up a rousing "Celebration" that had nearly every person in the place crowding onto the dance floor.

He caught his bride around the waist. And giggling like young new lovers, they snuck out.

Because.

Consummating awaited.

* * * * *

Don't miss
Faking It with a Fortune
by USA TODAY *bestselling author Michelle Major,*
the first installment in the new continuity
The Fortunes of Texas: Secrets of Fortune's Gold Ranch
On sale February 2025, wherever Harlequin books
and ebooks are sold!

And catch up with The Fortunes of Texas:
Fortune's Secret Children:

Fortune's Secret Marriage
by Jo McNally

Nine Months to a Fortune
by New York Times *bestselling author Elizabeth Bevarly*

Fortune's Faux Engagement
by Carrie Nichols

A Fortune Thanksgiving
by Michelle Lindo-Rice

Fortune's Holiday Surprise
by Jennifer Wilck

Available now!